DARTWOOD'S DAUGHTERS

Also by Rebecca Baldwin
Arabella and the Beast

DARTWOOD'S DAUGHTERS

Rebecca Baldwin

St. Martin's Press / New York

Library of Congress Cataloging-in-Publication Data

Baldwin, Rebecca.
    Dartwood's daughters / Rebecca Baldwin.
        p.   cm.
    ISBN 0-312-02898-9
    I. Title.
    PS3552.A4515D37 1989
    813'.54—dc19   89-4105
                                                        CIP

First Edition

10 9 8 7 6 5 4 3 2 1

in memory of Barbara Salomon

Chapter One

THE RAIN, WHICH HAD sputtered across the landscape for a fortnight, had ceased. A brief spell of warmth and sunshine had bathed the Cotswolds all morning, bringing the world into summer bloom.

Dartwood House, a solid-looking brick structure dating back to the days of Queen Anne, seemed that morning to be particularly lovely. It was nestled among gardens and plantings that had been carefully laid down by its late mistress, Lady Dartwood, whose reputation as a notable gardener was still spoken of with awe in horticultural circles, more than a decade after her death. Beneath the care of her dour Scots gardener, still employed by Sir August Dartwood, roses bloomed in pink and red and white; lilacs and phlox splashed purple hues against the neatly clipped boxwood topiaries. The lover's knots borders of santolina and rosemary were just beginning to put forth blossoms, while the thyme that surrounded the sundial was again threatening to run riot into the pansy beds around the gravel pathways.

With a blast from the postboy's horn, the smart post chaise rounded the brick gateposts of the entrance and began its course up the raked gravel drive. A young lady in a simple sprig muslin round dress, her fair complexion and flaming red hair concealed beneath the protection of an ever-so-slightly faded chip-straw leghorn, raised her eyes from the basket of Malmaison roses she was carrying in one arm. She looked utterly reassured, as if some intuition had been proven correct.

"Now, Miss Amy, who can that be?" MacDowell, the gardener, asked. He was slightly annoyed at this interruption in his discourse. He was not paid, he was fond of saying, the princely sum of forty pounds a year to interest himself in the comings and goings of the household. He resented anyone who would take him away from conversations about horticulture with his favourite among the daughters of his late and adored mistress. On such a glorious day, when decisions had to be made on the summer plantings in the Shakespeare Garden, the visitor would no doubt pen her up indoors. From beneath his beetling brows, he glared furiously at the yellow post chaise as it pulled up smartly before the portico, the sweating, snorting team scattering his well-raked gravel in all directions.

"Why, MacDowell," Miss Amelia Dartwood said in her soft voice, "it is Miss Eve, come home from Italy. I wonder that she did not write to tell us to expect her!"

MacDowell opened and closed his mouth, but said nothing, merely watching in amazement as, without another word, Miss Amelia Dartwood thrust her cutting basket into his hands and picked up her skirts, making her way down the oak moss path toward the portico.

"Now how in the world did she know that? How do those two always seem to know about each other?" MacDowell mused aloud, stroking his mustache and shaking his head.

Sure enough, as the coachman jumped down from the box, and in a gesture anyone of the postilions and outriders could have told an observer was a mark of high favour indeed, let down the steps and opened the door with his own hand, a fashionably dressed lady in the latest Continental style emerged from inside the chaise. From the silk roses in her lacquered straw bonnet to the sateen bands on her Pomona green carriage pelisse, she was the very picture of elegance as she accepted the coachman's hand and stepped to the ground to stand blinking in the sunlight, her head automatically turning toward the rose garden from whence Amy was emerging, arms opened wide.

When she saw Miss Amelia Dartwood coming toward her, the lady's smile was like the sun coming out from behind the clouds, and she hurried toward her, removing her bonnet as she did so.

In the fervour of their embrace, Amy's leghorn slipped from her hair and hung down her back on its ribbons, and the onlooking personnel of the Bristol Transport Company gaped in astonishment.

"Glory be!" said the coachman, tilting back his high-crowned beaver to scratch his head. "Them two be as like to each other as two peas in the same pod! Did you ever see the like?"

"Well, of course they be alike," MacDowell said gruffly, coming up behind Amy at a more leisurely pace.

"Them's ye Dartwood twins, Miss Eve an' Miss Amy—they're identical twins!"

They made an affecting picture as they stood and embraced, for indeed they were alike in every respect nature had given them. Both had heads of flaming, lustrous hair, although it could be seen that Amy's had been cropped short and was now growing in again, while Eve's was wound about her head in two long braids. They were both a little above the medium in height, with the same high-waisted, long-limbed figures.

Both had large green eyes set beneath straight, almost startled dark brows, and slightly retroussé noses above delicate rosebud mouths, placed in twin oval faces. While the prevailing fashion was, as it almost always was, against red hair and milky skin, it would have taken sterner critics than these to call the Dartwood sisters plain and gingery.

"You didn't write," Amy said accusingly to her sister, "and tell us you were coming. Mrs. Murdoch thought I was quite mad when I said last week that your bedroom should be turned out and the Holland covers taken up. How is Papa?"

Eve laughed and shook her head, drinking in the sight of the sister from whom she had been separated for what seemed like an eternity. They had never been apart for eighteen hours before, let alone eighteen months. "Twin sense!" she exclaimed. "I knew that you would know when I was coming, you see, just as I knew I had to come home a little early because you needed me for some reason."

They looked at each other for a moment. Although no outsider could have possibly understood, the bond between them was so strong that one could intuit, with some twin-given sixth sense, the other's thoughts. It was never very strong, and frequently the intuition was murky or nonexistent, but it had been a feature of their lives since birth, and neither tended to consider it anything other than normal. Eve smiled and touched her sister's cheek affectionately. "Papa is fine, and he sends his love, and he will be home in about six weeks give or take, and wait until you see what he has sent you from Naples, and you cannot use your twin sense—it must be a surprise! But what is it that I feel disturbing you, sister? Something is amiss, and I must know what it is!"

Amy touched her short curls ruefully, and made a slight shrug, as if it were nothing. But in the depths of her eyes, her sister read a troubled expression, and was not comforted.

But before they could exchange any confidences, however brief, a plump woman in a lawn morning cap and a drab tartan round gown emerged from the doorway, a shawl thrown over her shoulders and the cook's menu still in her hand. Although she was of middle years and had a somewhat prim and spinsterly countenance, with a pair of spectacles perched upon her long, thin nose, her expression was illuminated by a certain good humour in the large brown eyes and the wide smile on her lips.

"Eve!" she exclaimed. "When Amy said that she knew you would be home soon, I thought it was merely her imagination, but here you are! My dear child!"

"Tabby!" Eve cried joyfully, and embraced the older woman so strongly that the latter gave a great gasp.

"My dear child, there is no need for violence, you know!" she remonstrated in a tone that could only have come from a governess to an erstwhile charge, but she was nonetheless happy to see the returning daughter. "Dear me, you are as brown as a berry! That will not do at all! It will be buttermilk and borax baths for your complexion and hands tonight! Did you go out into that hot sun without so much as a hat and gloves and a parasol against all advice?"

Eve laughed. "Indeed I did, but it would be impossible to do otherwise when one is engaged in sifting through layers and layers of volcanic ash and dirt! Only wait until you see what antiquities Papa has managed to send back for his collections—some of his discoveries were quite remarkable!"

Miss Tabith Fisher pushed her spectacles up on her nose again and peered myopically at the twins. "I trust your father is well, then?" she asked.

Eve nodded. "Having a wonderful time! Oh, you have no idea what Naples is like, Tabby! But then of course neither does Papa, for he lives and breathes only for his excavations, and we might have been on the other side of the moon for all that he cared. It was quite, quite decadent, I assure you!" This was said purely with the intention of shocking Miss Fisher, but Miss Fisher had not been with the Dartwood twins for fifteen years and more to be so easily quizzed.

"Yes, I daresay," she replied absently. "One does think of abroad as being somewhat decadent. Dear Papa was always in Paris, you know . . . however, my dear, we must not stand here and keep you on tenderhooks!"

"Oh, no, for I must particularly supervise the unloading of the chaise, you know! I brought what I could with me, and the larger crates will be coming from Portsmouth by carter. It was a long journey home, you see, but I did manage to arrive in one piece, and I am most anxious to see that all of Papa's antiquities survived in the same condition—"

6

"Eve!" Amy exclaimed in shock. "You did not come from Italy all by yourself?"

Eve laughed, shaking her head. "I may be the hoydenish twin, but I promise you I am not so sunk into impropriety as to travel unescorted, particularly with this Bonaparte person rattling his sabres! No, I had the company of Leon Shelldrake all the way back, and a more Friday-faced individual, or a more respectable escort no female could wish to have. I endured him as far as Oxford, and I think he was as glad to be rid of me as I was him! I am sure that Papa's dealer must be an excellent sort of man, but one only need look at Mrs. Shelldrake and all those little Shelldrakes to know that he is *not* the most fascinating of travel companions! Seasick out and roadsick from Portsmouth, but I do see his point that England is best and abroad is sometimes terrible." She dismissed the highly proper Mr. Shelldrake with a wave of her hand, and if Amy and Miss Fisher both felt Mr. Shelldrake must have been as glad to allow his charge to come the last five miles to Dartwood without him as she had been to divest herself of his company, they were far too happy to have her all to themselves to say anything disloyal.

"Anyway," Eve continued quickly, "Papa was most anxious that Shelldrake return to Oxford, for on Saturday, you know, there is the Grinling auction at King's, and Papa is most anxious that Mr. Shelldrake bid for him on that Etruscan statuette—but here is MacDowell and all the staff come to greet me!"

From the bowels of the house, the servants were pouring forth to welcome home the returning daughter. Most of them had known her since infancy, and it was fully a quarter of an hour before she could finish greeting them all, set MacDowell and his men to unloading the crates and the trunks from the chaise, direct them to be placed in the ballroom for the time being, thank and discharge the coachman and the postilions to the kitchen quarters for food and strong ale.

An hour later, with a sigh, she was easing herself into a shoe tub of hot water, carried up from the kitchen in copper kettles by the scullery maid.

"Of the two things I desire most in this world at this minute, a hot bath and some food, I think the bath is by far the better," she remarked, splashing a bit in the rose-water suds. "You have no idea how one yearns for a hot bath when all one has to clean with is an ewer of water and a basin. Abroad is not always as clean a place as one could wish."

Amy had settled herself on the end of her sister's bed, leaning against one of the four tester posts. From a tray of tea and bread and cold meat on the chair before her, she selected a bit of ham and placed it on a piece of bread, handing it to her sister before she was asked.

Neither twin thought this an odd gesture, and Eve accepted this bit of food with wet fingers, munching hungrily. Amy smiled.

In the next room, Jane, the maid both girls had shared until Eve's departure for Naples, was unpacking her bandboxes and trunks with much rustling of silver paper and many exclamations on the latest additions to Miss Dartwood's wardrobe from foreign parts, dismay or approval expressed with many *tch's* and *mmm's*.

Eve popped the last bit of bread and cheese into her mouth and submerged her head. When she came up, she reached for the soap and began to lather her hair.

"But that's enough war stories for now," Eve said,

lathering with strong fingers. "Tell me what is going on here. Is Aunt Seale on one of her tears?"

Amy sighed, lacing her fingers together and examining the toes of her shoes beneath the ruffles of her gown. "Well, Aunt Seale is involved in it, yes," she finally admitted.

"I might have known," Eve exclaimed. "What crackbrained scheme has she come up with now?"

Just as their old governess Tabby was their support and mainstay, and they could not have imagined life without her at Dartwood House, so their fraternal aunt and neighbor, Lady Seale, was the bane of their existence.

From the time of their mother's death, Aunt Seale had attempted to sweep down from Seale Abbey, just above the hill, and undertake to manage their lives. Like many childless women, she imagined herself an expert on child-raising, and many long and tedious hours had been spent (wasted, Eve thought) in the drawing room at Seale Abbey learning how to pour tea, curtsey like wheat before the wind, *glide* not *gallop*, and do a thousand tiny, torturous stitches in embroidery samples of surpassing mediocrity, at least on Eve's part. Amy, always sweet and docile, had submitted to these visits with the same attention and care she'd devoted to Miss Fisher's schoolroom lessons, and horrors, had actually seemed to enjoy them. But Eve had always performed with one eye out the window, yearning with all her heart to be riding, playing battledore and shuttlecock, fishing, or doing any one of a hundred things in the sunshine and the shadows of the woods, where she knew there were foxes' dens and badger holes and a lovely green pond awaiting her.

To be utterly fair to Lady Seale, that estimable

female was under absolutely no illusions as to her brother's abilities as a father. While no man could have been fonder of his offspring than Sir August, there could also have been no man any vaguer in his day-to-day attitudes about the raising of daughters, or indeed any other worldly subject. Sir August, like many another scholar, seemed to live entirely in his own world, and to be upon better terms with Suetonius and Pericles than the members of his own household. While Lady Seale would have been the last person in Oxford to deny her brother's undisputed brilliance as an antiquarian, scholar and collector of classical objects, or to denigrate his reputation as a gentleman archaeologist, she was also wise enough to see that without the aid of an influential female (and Lady Seale was nothing if not influential) her nieces would dwindle away into spinsterhood. While she considered the academic influence of Miss Fisher in their lives as all very well and necessary, she could not help but deplore the decidedly bluestockinged teachings of that lady's skill. To know Greek, Latin, Italian, French, mathematics, history, and literature might well be useful in these dangerously modern times when female education was much in vogue, but to the mind of Lady Seale, such female skills as the ability to sketch in crayons and watercolors, to sew a neat stitch and to be able to acquit oneself credibly on the dance floor were far more likely to win a girl a husband than the ability to discourse, in flawless French, upon the mistresses of Louis XIV.

To bring the twins out credibly in London was the sum ambition of her life. With only five hundred pounds a year apiece and that deplorable red hair, she foresaw only trouble ahead if they were not suitably married to fine and decent gentlemen. Gold balls and coronets she believed were far above their touch, but she did hope that, after three Seasons in Town, the Dartwood twins might have fixed their affections upon a pair of worthy gentlemen. When this failed to happen, she was depressed, and retreated to Oxford again in defeat.

It was not that the Dartwood twins were not popular. Indeed, two lovely young ladies alike as two peas in a pod were bound to attract favourable attention, even amid the competition of the London marriage market. But unfortunately, neither twin was inclined to marry without at least some feeling of attachment toward her future husband, and although at least one or two gentlemen came up to snuff, Amy and Eve had been so far unmoved as to continue to prefer their single state to a marriage without love.

To Lady Seale's way of thinking, this matter of love was an entirely modern notion, and one that such a sensible female as Miss Fisher should have nipped in the bud, or at the very least, in the schoolroom. Sir August, when applied to for parental assistance, was content to mutter that the girls gave him no harm at home, and indeed were a great help to him in his studies, so why should he wish to see them married off when they did not wish to be?

This reply of course infuriated his sister no end, and might have caused a permanent schism between Seale Abbey and Dartwood House had not Sir August received about that time an invitation from his old crony Sir William Hamilton, ambassador to the Kingdom of the Two Sicilies and a passionate antiquarian in his own right, to come to Naples to excavate, with the gracious permission of King Ferdinand and Queen Maria Carolina, a Pompeiian villa recently discovered in the shadow of that ancient volcano.

Fortunately, Sir William had married his mistress of

longstanding, the beautiful and legendary Mrs. Hart, so there could be no objection on moral grounds of taking along the twins. And Lady Seale might be able to console herself with the thought that while the court of Ferdinand and Maria Carolina was hardly the most moral place for two young ladies to be presented, Naples itself was so entirely fashionable a place for the English abroad that there might be some hope in the idea that one or the other of the twins might contract an alliance there.

Eve and Amy, past their twentieth summer, were under far less illusion about the way in which the world operated than their aunt might have wished to believe, and of course Eve was delighted with the idea of visiting a new place. Unhappily, a month before they were to depart, the twins contracted influenza. Eve, always the stronger of the two, threw it off in a week. But Amy, whose constitution was always more delicate, seemed to linger in illness, never quite incapacitated and never quite well either, so that upon the advice of the doctor, she was left behind while Eve forged on to Italy with Sir August.

This venture marked the first time the twins had been separated for more than a fortnight since birth, and they were not unnaturally inclined to view their parting with some anxiety.

Older by twenty minutes, Eve had always been outgoing and adventurous, perhaps, in the eyes of Aunt Seale, too much so. After three seasons of containment in the drawing rooms of London, forced, beneath Aunt Seale's sharp eye, to comport herself in the most insipid entertainments, she viewed a trip to Naples as high adventure as well as welcome release.

Amy, younger and quieter than her sister, had also found their three London seasons to be a trial, but for her they had been exhausting. Her natural manner was retiring, and her deepest pleasures were found in home and hearth and the company of familiar friends. For her, a journey to Italy might have been a voyage to the moon, and it was not unnatural for her to linger in convalescence, in dread of going abroad with a frail constitution.

Eve would not have left her twin behind had she believed that Amy might need her at Dartwood House. But she sensed correctly that Amy's real terror was of facing yet another unknown. Eve should—indeed, she *must*—go ahead, Amy insisted, and so Eve did, while Amy stayed at home with Tabby and Aunt Seale to look after her.

Although letters had sped back and forth between Dartwood and Naples, and their special twin sense continued unabated by distance, now that they were reunited each had the small and uneasy feeling that the other had passed through experiences that had subtly changed her, drawing the twins apart a little distance.

How this should affect them it was too soon to tell. And besides, Eve was full to bursting with the news of Mr. Thomas Perry.

"Of course, I wrote to you all about meeting him at the Hamiltons. Well, you might think it quite strange that Papa would take me there, considering Lady Hamilton's dubious background, but you see, abroad is so much different from home, and besides, the Queen of Naples is quite her bosom bow, so it's all considered perfectly proper. But before I left he spoke to me, and when Papa comes back, we mean to announce our engagement. You will like him, Amy, I know you will, and I think even Papa must come to see his good points when he understands that my mind is quite made up. Thomas promised that he would speak most particularly to Papa on the subject as soon as he had a chance, but I must warn you, my love, that Thomas is a poet, and doesn't think like ordinary people. And you know what Papa's like, so I am left to hope that they will understand, each one, what the conversation is all about when the time comes. For you know, Papa can be so vague sometimes, particularly when he's very deep into one of his delvings that he barely notes what goes on in this century. I fear Thomas is a bit like Papa in that sense himself, although he does pay attention to one when one begs him most particularly to do so. He has written an ode to my eyes, which I think is very pretty, but then I am not the admirer of poetry that you are. But he does teach at Cambridge, which is why we never met him before, and he has three thousand pounds a year of his own, so I daresay Papa cannot object on that account." She lifted a foot from the bubbles and examined it critically. "I am not all that brown," Eve mused, continuing on, "oh, Amy, Thomas is so handsome, of course I was attracted to him at once, but I have to admit, just to you, that he will take as much managing as Papa, for like Papa he tends to live with his head in the clouds, but I can change that soon enough, I assure you; just as soon as we are engaged I intend—"

But looking up, she saw that her sister was not attending to her at all, but rather looking out the window with such misery written upon her pretty face that it was clear she was all but consumed with anxiety.

"Dear Amy, what sort of unnatural sister am I?" Eve demanded, quickly reaching for a towel on the slipper chair beside her and rising from the tub. "Here I am prattling on and on about my happiness when you are consumed with *un*happiness of the worst sort!"

Amy made a vague gesture with her hand and attempted a smile that failed to reach her eyes. "Oh, no," she said weakly. "I am of course most anxious to hear

14

about your Thomas. I am sure that if you love him, I will learn to do so! Indeed, he must be a paragon of all virtues—oh, Eve! I am so miserable! I know not which way to turn, and I fear the worst!"

In a moment, Eve had wrapped her robe about her and was sitting on the edge of the bed beside her sister, somewhat damp but nonetheless there, her arm about the frailer twin's shoulders, her tone that of absolutely no nonsense.

"Here, here, now, I am home, and whatever it is, I am sure that we can find some way to solve it. Has Aunt Seale been plaguing you again? Drat the woman!"

"Oh, Eve, you must not say so! After Aunt Seale has been so good to us!" Amy said reproachfully. "She *means* well."

"She means to marry us both off come hell or high water, and no matter to what or whom! I for one, am glad I have relieved her of myself, for I am perfectly certain that she will disapprove of Thomas, as she would of any man not of her level of society! So, what has Aunt Seale done now to put you into a pother?"

"Nothing really. That is, she means well, of course—but I cannot—oh, dear!"

One large and perfect tear fell from Amy's eye and coursed down her cheek. Unlike her sister, she could cry without in the least affecting her looks.

"Now, now," Eve said bracingly, "Don't become a watering pot, I pray you! Now what happened to put you into such a pother, my love?"

Amy dabbed at her eyes with a handkerchief. "Well, about a month ago, Aunt Seale decided to take me to Bath—I wrote you a letter about the trip, but I suppose you did not receive it before you left?"

Eve shook her head. "No doubt it is only now arriv-

15

ing. That nasty little Bonaparte makes so much trouble in Europe that everything is delayed. So you went to Bath with Aunt Seale. To take the waters, no doubt, and see what eligible gentlemen were about!"

"To take the waters only!" Amy assured her. "I believe she had quite made up her mind that I should dwindle into an old maid, you see, and things were much more peaceful after that!"

It was upon the tip of Eve's tongue to remark that Aunt Seale's character was not one that would give into fate so easily, but she restrained herself.

"At first I enjoyed it immensely, for you know Bath is not at all like London, and everything is done very slowly and comfortably, and one is never thrown into a pother trying to think of some witty rejoiner or put to the blush because one's style is not fashion and dash. Aunt took rooms for us at the White Hart, which is the first style of luxury in Bath, and every morning we went to the Pump Room so I could drink the waters. Eve! Tuppence a glass, drawn by this terrible old woman, and such an awful taste! I cannot see that it did me the least bit of good, but everyone swears by them, you know, so every morning I downed a nasty glass. And then in the afternoon, you know, we would have a little rest and some luncheon, and Aunt and I would shop a bit on Milsom Street, and look in at Hookham's Library. And then, of course, dinner, and then in the evenings the Assemblies, which were very nice, not at all like Almack's where one was terrified of the patronesses, but one could dance, you know and have ices and drink lovely orangeat punch, and it was exactly in the style I most like."

"It sounds terribly slow to me," Eve said with a laugh, hugging her sister, "but yes, it does sound exactly what you would like, my love! But what happened there to upset you so?"

Amy bit her lower lip and looked downcast. "Well, you see, at first I didn't think it was so terrible, but then later, when I realized that it was all wrong, it was too late!" She wrung her hands. "And now he's coming to stay with Aunt Seale, and she says he means to offer for me, and I would be a fool to turn him down because I shall never have another chance, and even if I did, it would never match this one, and I should be the happiest female in England, I know, but I am not! I am miserable, because he terrifies me!"

"Who? Who is this man?" Eve asked, ready to go forth and slay the monster who made her sister weep at once.

"L-Lord Barras is his name," Amy said woefully.

Eve raised one eyebrow. "You mean the collector? The one who's always jauntering off somewhere to excavate some ancient ruin? Why, he must be quite as old as Papa!"

Amy shook her head. "He's not old at all, no more than thirty, I suppose, and he's quite handsome, but oh, Eve, he is so cold and so aloof and arrogant that he quite terrifies me! I cannot marry him! I cannot! But Aunt Seale says I must because he is quite rich, and besides, Papa will be so pleased with the match!"

Eve's head was swimming a little, but she was used to excavating the truth from her sister's roundaboutations. "Calmly, calmly! First of all, you know that Papa would never wish you to marry anyone you did not want to, even if it were Pliny himself! Papa may be a classicist, but he is not a Roman parent, thank God!" she exclaimed, stroking her sister's shoulder soothingly. "Now, how did you come to meet this Lord Barras, and whatever gave him the idea that you were in the least interested in accepting his proposal? I detect Aunt Seale's hand in all of this!"

Amy shook her head miserably. "It wasn't Aunt Seale's fault! Well, not really, but you can see, can't you, how she would leap at a chance to see me well settled with a man who is rich as Croesus, and handsome and from an excellent family! It is a far better match than I might ever be expected to make, especially since we have been out three seasons without an offer, Aunt Seale says. But while I *know* that I cannot expect to marry where I feel love, still—he frightens me!"

"He must be a monster! Whatever did he do? Has he tried to make violent love to you? Or threatened you in some way? Only tell me at once!"

Amy shook her head. "No, no, none of that! He has always been a perfect gentleman! It is only that his manners are so very grand, and his attitude so cold—indeed, I have found him so intimidating that I was certain that he would not think twice about me after we left Bath, but now, you see, Aunt says he intends to offer for me, and I know not what to do! I was so afraid of him, Eve, that when he asked if he might press his suit, I was too overcome to do more than make some little noise, and I fear he took it as an assent!"

"What?" Eve now felt definitely dizzy, and she had to take a moment to straighten herself out before she could continue. "Let us start at the beginning. How did you meet him?"

"Didn't I explain that? No, I guess I did not. Oh, dear, I have been so upset by all of this that I am quite flummoxed I fear. You know that I have never been in the least good at handling crises . . ." Fresh tears threatened, and Eve quickly interrupted them with a brisk exclamation.

"Fudge! You are simply shy, that's all, and so sweet-natured that you are liable to be taken advantage of by people like Aunt Seale and this Lord What's His Name. Amy, you did not encourage him, did you?"

"Oh, how can you ask me such a thing? Of course I did not. That is, not *intentionally*. Oh, Eve, you don't think that he thought I was *flirting* with him, do you?" Amy asked, genuinely horrified.

"With men, it is always hard to tell," Eve replied darkly. "One is merely *civil* to them and they presume there is a great deal more to it than mere politeness. Men, you know, have vast oceans of conceit that no female would ever dream of possessing! Now, my love, tell me how you met this person. And from the beginning."

Amy licked her lips, thinking hard. It was not that she was unintelligent; indeed, her understanding was most superior in matters of literature and history and art. It was only when it came to her fellow creatures that she was liable to be tripped up. "Well, he was at the Assembly, and asked to be made known to me, you see, as he knew who Papa was. And it turned out that Aunt Seale went to school with his mama, so that was all right."

"I can just imagine," Eve murmured, but Amy was impervious to sarcasm.

"So, I stood up with him once or twice at the Assemblies. But he stood up with so many other ladies, too, that it made no difference to me. Eve, it is the most wonderful thing that you can imagine not to lack for partners! I barely noted him then, you see. But then he started to come to call upon Aunt Seale and I, and that of course I could not like, for he had a way of making me feel so—so countrified and awkward, you see, as if he were always laughing at me. But Aunt adores him—you will see—and soon he was escorting us to the Wells and even once took us to see his estate, Highgrove. If I had known then what his intentions were, I should have fainted. It was such a very grand place, you know, one of the stately old homes of England, full of treasures and these vast, depressing old salons, exactly like Seale Abbey only more so, and the butler was as grand as the Prince Regent! Only think of having to preside over *that*!" Amy shuddered eloquently. She placed the tip of her finger into her mouth nervously. "Of course at the time, I did not think of it, but we dined at a table set for three, large enough to seat twenty, and you may imagine how *that* was! Oh, Eve, I am so stupid, I never thought—I only assumed you know that since he was a friend of Aunt Seale's—or his mama had been a friend of Aunt Seale's, you know, that he was just being kind to two ladies visiting Bath. So you may imagine how I felt when, on our last night there, he took Aunt Seale and I to Sydney Gardens to see the fireworks displays, and when Aunt was talking with some friends at the next table, asked me if he might see me again. All I could do was make this sound, I was never so shocked in my life, and at that moment this enormous Catherine Wheel went off right above our heads and I suppose he took it for an assent. At any rate," she finished gloomily, "he now plans to come and visit with Aunt Seale, and she says I am as good as engaged, as he intends to make me an offer."

"Well, all you have to do is tell him he mistook your intentions," Eve pointed out sensibly.

"That's what Tabby says. But you have no idea how frightening he can be!" Amy wailed.

"Tell me," Eve said, trying to maintain a sense of

calm rationality, "precisely what did he say to you and what did you say to him?"

Amy swallowed hard. "He said 'Miss Dartwood, I hope you will allow me to call upon you when I am in Oxford in June,' and I said something like 'Awp!'"

"'Awp?'"

"'Awp!'" Amy repeated miserably. "At that moment, this great Catherine Wheel went off, you see, and I was *so* startled! Aunt of course says that no gentleman would ask a lady to allow him to call if his intentions were not very serious and that an *awp* is as good as a *yes* and an announcement in the *Post*! And further, that having assented to allowing him to call, I have as good as accepted his proposal, and that to cry off would not only be shabby, it would be dishonourable, as well as positively foolish, since Lord Barras is one of the most elusive bachelors in Britain!"

"And I also imagine she said a great deal more," Eve said dryly. "Was there ever such a female as Aunt? I swear, if Bonaparte himself proposed, she would like as not have us marry him, if only to be married!"

"Eve, Aunt Seale has been most good to us!" Amy protested in shock.

"Yes, yes, and yes, that I cannot deny! But however kind her intentions are, you must admit that her way of *managing* everything leaves something to be desired!"

Since Eve was every bit as managing—in her own fashion—as her aunt, Amy only smiled and kept silent. Now that her sister was here, she was certain that all would be happily resolved, and so great was Eve's confidence in her own ability to tackle and conquer that she did nothing to disabuse her sister of this happy notion.

"Well, we shall contrive something, I assure you!

Only imagine the effrontery of this man! I suppose he is so bloated with his own self-esteem that he thinks he need only be kind to a chit before she will fall willingly into his schemes! And why, pray tell, does he wish to be married at all? I would think, from what you say and from what I have heard, that this Lord Barras would be far too grand for anything but the daughter of a duke!"

"He feels, Aunt says, that he must needs marry and produce an heir To the estate and title, and that a daughter of Sir August Dartwood would bring a handsome dowry of ancient antiquities to add to his collections, Papa having no male heirs."

A crease appeared between Eve's brows, and her chin went up. "Highly romantic! A fine wooing indeed! Doubtless he saves his fine words and demonstrations of affection and respect for his mistresses, of which I understand he has had a great many!"

"Eve!" Amy exclaimed, profoundly embarrassed.

Miss Dartwood had the grace to shrug. "Well, I know that unmarried ladies are not supposed to know about mistresses and such, but one of course does, and there's no point in putting any sort of roundaboutations on it, it's a known fact! *All* gentlemen have mistresses! Except Thomas of course, his mind is far too exalted for such things."

"But there is worse yet. He—he told Aunt that I should not make him such a very bad wife, once I was broke to bridle!"

If Eve had needed an excuse to work herself into an indignant rage, this last remark provided it for her. "Broke to bridle! Broke to bridle! How dare he speak so of a Dartwood of Dartwood House?" she demanded, springing up from the bed and pacing the room in a high dungeon, shaking with anger. "As if you were a horse!

The arrogance of this man surpasses all bounds! He should be horsewhipped!"

"Oh, dear," Amy murmured, uncertain, as usual, what to do with her sister in one of these moods.

Fortunately, at that moment Miss Fisher appeared in the doorway, an elegant woolen shawl draped over her bottle-green round gown.

"My dear Eve, what a lovely gift you have brought me—" she began, and then, understanding the scene into which she had stumbled, added without the least trace of surprise, "Ah, I apprehend Amy has been telling you about Lord Barras."

"Oh, Tabby!" Eve cried, "where were you when all this was happening? For I know that you would have put a period to this folly before it got out of hand!"

Miss Fisher's expression did not change in the least. Impervious for the most part to the moods and mischief of her erstwhile charges, blessed with an unshakable degree of placid commonsense, she had always been the one person who could restrain the twins from their worst mischief.

From the moment of her arrival, she had been the only person in the household who could, without effort, distinguish one from the other.

"If I apprehend that you are speaking about Amy's experiences in Bath, then I must tell you that I was not invited to make up one of the party, as I was visiting my sister in Yarmouth."

"Besides, Aunt said there wasn't enough room in her old carriage for her, me, her maid, her majordomo and all her things, let alone Tabby."

"Be that as it may, I would certainly never suggest that Lady Seale wished to restrain me from joining the company," Tabby said. "As you know, I always have a fortnight with my sister in May."

"But what say you to all of this?" Eve asked. She sank into the chaise by the window and propped her chin into her hand, regarding Tabby thoughtfully.

Miss Fisher, satisfied that Eve was at least willing to listen to a rational voice, shook her head placidly. "For myself, I would refrain from judging Lord Barras until I had met him. Too often, the impressions of another are not those we receive ourselves. However, since Amy has taken an aversion to him, I cannot help but feel that any attempt to pursue a course of marriage with him would be a great mistake at this time."

"It all reeks of Aunt Seale's fine Italian hand," Eve fumed, mixing metaphors with a carelessness that made her erstwhile mentor wince in resignation.

"I of course, will not say anything against Lady Seale. She is an estimable woman whose virtues are many, and her concern for her nieces has been most evident. However, like many persons who are childless, or do not deal directly with children as a part of their profession, she assumes a great many things that are ultimately incorrect, however good her intentions. It is true, alas, that a spinster does not fare too happily in our society, however," she added dryly.

The twins both turned at once. "Tabby, do we treat you badly? Oh, say it is not so!" They both chorused at once.

Miss Fisher was swift to allay their fears, taking their hands into her own. "No, no of course—I could not have hoped for better treatment than I have received at Dartwood House. Believe me, that I am very fond of both of you, as fond as I am of my own nieces and nephews, and well, no one could have been a more thoughtful or considerate employer than Sir August."

Had they not been involved in their own dilemmas, the Dartwood sisters might have detected a faint blush appearing in Miss Fisher's spinsterly cheeks, and an even fainter smile flickering across her impassive countenance. It was gone in the flicker of an eyelash, however, and when she spoke again she was as brisk and businesslike as always.

"I shall admit that the approaching visit of this Lord Barras has cast poor Amy quite into the depths, however, and that I do not like to see, especially since she has so much improved in health of late. I think that your *twin sense* was most wise in compelling you to return home, Eve, when it did."

She was one of the few persons who accepted without question the bond that existed between the twins, primarily because she had had frequent opportunity to see it in effect.

"Well, we shall think of something, never fear," Eve announced briskly, patting her sister's hand. "But for now, I think that I am like to die of starvation. Tabby, can the cook find something for me to eat?"

Chapter
Two

IT WAS PLEASANT TO hear laughter again emerging from the sunny yellow morning room, where the twins had staked out their own special provenance.

Of all the rooms in Dartwood House, it was the most cheerful and the least adorned with fine and priceless examples of Sir August's mania for the treasures of the ancient world; but even here, a piece of a marble head rested against the mantel clock and a trivet that had supported an oil lamp in the times of the Caesars stood in one corner, irreverently draped, with an afghan Miss Fisher sometimes spread over her knees when she took a drowse on cold winter afternoons.

By contrast to these items, the rest of the furnishings of the room were positively modern, although most of

them dated back to the reign of Queen Anne and were comfortably worn and a little shabby with generations of use.

When Sir August's father, the late baronet, had employed this room as the study in which he wrote learned treatises upon the Beaker People of early Britain, it must have been a colder and more scholarly place, but neither Eve nor Amy could endure long without comfortable chairs, their clutter and cushions; since earliest days, this had been their room, and their room it had remained through the years, until gradually it had achieved a decidedly more feminine aspect, being full of half-completed pieces of various projects and books and magazines one or the other happened to be engaged upon reading at some particular moment.

Of a consequence, it was a pleasant, female jumble of a room. When they were small, it had been the twins' sanctuary from a world of adults, and now it was a sanctuary from having to be grownups themselves.

The fire in the marble hearth was dead, but a bouquet of roses in a Delft pagoda stood on the table, and the windows were opened to receive the full benefit of an English summer.

A cold luncheon of beef, cheese, and bread having been eagerly devoured, Eve was now helping herself to the next-to-last macaroon on the plate and laughing as she reminisced about the childhood antics she and Amy had contrived.

"D'you recall how no one could ever tell us apart," she was saying to Miss Fisher, who sat placidly in the corner in her chair, a bit of tatting work in her lap. "So of course we were forever showing up in one place or another, passing ourselves off as the other. We quite drove Tallant mad sometimes, you know. I am surprised he did

not give his notice after he saw Amy on the landing, and then a second or two later in the kitchen snitching delicious macaroons from good Mrs. Beckley, who never gave us away."

Amy nodded. "We were very wicked, you know," she said softly.

"Of course it was all my idea. Amy was always so good!" Eve cried. "But then you came and we behaved. You civilised us!"

Regarding them over her spectacles, Miss Fisher was once again struck by how very similar the twins were, even when unconscious of their twinship. Even now, as they sat at opposite sides of the table, they were both making the same gestures toward the macaroons. With their other hands, each propped up her chin, and beneath the cloth their legs were both neatly crossed at the ankles, and their spines both curved in the same posture.

"Of course, *you* could always tell us apart," Eve was saying. "No one else could, not even Papa—especially not Papa, and certainly not Aunt Seale! Indeed, Aunt Seale still cannot tell us apart!"

"We were wont to plague her very sadly!" Amy said, sighing regretfully. "While Eve was out having my riding lesson, I would be in Aunt Seale's parlor doing her needlework!"

"So you see, I never made a sampler, and Amy can't ride a horse! Are we not deplorable?" Eve laughed, rolling her eyes.

"It was very wrong of you, yes," Miss Fisher said without any truly severe condemnation in her tone.

"But I think Aunt deserved it," Eve said mulishly, setting her jaw. "You know how managing she is, Tabby!"

"She means well," Amy said with a sigh. "And I be-

lieve we are both fond of her, even if Eve continues to deride her in conversation."

"Oh, I suppose Aunt Seale is just all right," Eve said briskly. "But you know, Amy, that if you were to tell her that you didn't wish to marry this Lord Barras, such megrims and manipulations and prostrations and hysterics as we would see—"

"Aunt is sadly adverse to having her will thwarted," Amy agreed gloomily. "Particularly when she has taken such a liking to Lord Barras."

"Then let *her* marry him!" Eve suggested, biting firmly into the last macaroon.

"Perhaps if *you* were to tell her—" Amy suggested hopefully.

"What! And endure her tears, megrims, and vapours? No, I thank you! A lifetime is not enough to build up an endurance for one of Aunt Seale's scenes!" Eve's face suddenly transformed with a grin that was almost impish. "Of course, I could convince her that I was you and you were me, you know—word does travel between House and Abbey, but not that fast!"

"Lady Seale is in Reading, purchasing new curtain rods for her breakfast parlour, but she will be back tomorrow. And there is very little that passes between here and there that does not reach her ears, sooner or later, however well-intentioned people might be," Miss Fisher pointed out reasonably.

"Very true," Eve agreed. "But you know that she could never tell us apart." She tapped a finger thoughtfully against her cheek. "In fact, no one could ever tell us apart when we weren't inclined to let them, except for you, Tabby—you always knew the difference at a glance."

"Eve, whatever are you thinking?" Miss Fisher asked uneasily.

Eve's eyes opened wide. "Only that I could be Amy and she could be Eve, and no one would ever know. *Particularly* this Lord Barras person, who has never seen me. Fancy, his lordship arriving in the Cotswolds all ready to break his intended bride to bridle—oh, the misery of the man!—only to find she's not a filly that breaks so easily! Give me a day with him, and I promise you, he'll turn right back to his grand estate in Bath, never to be seen again!"

"Eve! You cannot! You would not! Would it really work?" Amy said all in one breath.

"My dear Evelina, such conduct would hardly be proper!"

"Eve, you know that it would be impossible for me to condone such an action!" Miss Fisher exclaimed. "What a tangled web we weave when first we practise to deceive," she added gloomily.

Eve was quick to put her arms about her shoulders in an affectionate embrace. "Dearest, dearest Tabby! Without you, I know not what we would be! But please, try to understand that Amy and I are no longer schoolgirls. In fact," Eve said without so much as a blush, "Now that I have seen a little of the world, I know that deception is not always a very bad thing. Only look: everyone knows that Lady Hamilton was Sir William's mistress for years and years before he married her. When they were merely living together, everyone rather had to pretend that she didn't exist, but now that they are married, she finds herself in the most respectable circles. Even Her Majesty is Lady Hamilton's great and good friend."

"Be that as it may," Miss Fisher said, and pressed her

lips firmly together, "I am not a prude, I hope, but I fail to see how Lady Hamilton's irregular position has anything to do with a pair of well-brought-up, gently bred girls—well, girls no longer, but old enough to know the difference between right and wrong—deceiving a gentleman, and an aunt who has been quite good to both of you!"

"Oh, please, Tabby, just let Eve take care of Lord Barras," Amy pleaded. "You *know* that she can."

Miss Fisher shook her head again. "I know that nothing good ever comes of dishonesty. And, I know that every time Eve takes one of these notions into her head, disaster is close at hand!"

"Oh, Tabby, not that episode with the dancing master and the sheets and the long lost ghost of Dartwood House again! Amy and I were mere children then! We're quite grown up now, and besides, it all came about in the end, didn't it?"

"Still, I thought the man would die of fright on the spot! You were very wicked to do such a thing. Of course he was ever so pompous, I must say, and deserved a strong setdown!" A very thin trace of a smile appeared at the corner of the former governess's mouth in spite of herself, and the twins, recognising this sign that the thin end of the wedge had been inserted, quickly pressed their point homeward.

"Dearest Tabby, only picture what great unhappiness we shall be avoiding! Amy's life *ruined,* and I daresay mine also, for how could I be happy if Amy were not? Forced into an unhappy marriage all on a misunderstanding because of a Catherine Wheel in Sydney Gardens! You cannot wish to see poor Amy a miserable prisoner of a man who speaks of a wife being *broke to bridle* as if she were an unbroken mare! Really, you know an afternoon spent with me being disagreeable and insulting as only I can do will drive him away, this Lord Barras person, thinking himself the most fortunate person in the world *not* to have made an offer! Result, three saved and happy lives!" Eve gripped Tabby's hands between her own, and kneeling at Miss Fisher's feet, gazed imploringly up into her eyes.

At the same time, Amy approached from her flank, throwing her arms about Miss Fisher's shoulders. "Dear Tabby, please! Only you can help us!" she pleaded.

"Only for an afternoon, you say?" Miss Fisher asked, sighing with resignation.

"I should think a few hours in the company of a spoiled and sulking harridan would be enough for any man! You know I can contrive to give this odious Lord Barras such a dislike for me that he shall be only too glad to recall a pressing engagement on the other side of the country before the cat can lick her tongue!" Eve exclaimed. "Besides," she added, playing her trump card, "Papa would wish it so, you know he would."

Since, above all things, Miss Fisher admired and respected the opinions of Sir August Dartwood, she relented slightly. "Oh, very well. But I warn you, if this gets out of hand—"

"How could it possibly do so?" Eve asked. "After all, we are not children anymore, but women of the world. At least I am, having been abroad. Compared to some of the things Italian ladies do to their husbands, this is mild indeed. Why, it's rather like this opera I saw at the San Carlo, *Cosi Fan Tutti*—"

"Oh, Eve, it's not at all like Mozart," Amy said, shaking her head.

"Well, you see!" With a bounding gesture, Eve rose and pulled the pins from her hair. Scarlet and shining, it fell in cascades to the middle of her back. From the table, she picked up a pair of sewing shears, and before she could be stopped, she proceeded to hack away at the bright tresses.

Shocked, Amy and Miss Fisher watched as the shorn hair rained about the floor around the impetuous twin. They were startled into inaction for several moments.

Indeed, it was a startling sacrifice for one who had always been so inordinately vain of her hair, as was Eve Dartwood.

A little afraid and a little defiant, she stopped, looking at their expressions, holding the shears between her fingers in a hand that just barely trembled.

"Oh, heavens," Amy sighed, rising to her feet. "That's no way to go about it, Eve. Tabby, hand me that shawl, I will drape it over her shoulders. Eve, you are a goose, but I do love you for this. Now, sit down and let me trim your hair *à la Méduse,* and we shall be as alike as two peas in a pod."

Obediently, Eve did as her sister told her, and in a quarter hour, the two of them stood gazing at their twin reflections in the mirror over the mantelpiece.

"As alike as two peas in a pod," Eve repeated, touching the weightlessness of her new soft curls where once her hair had hung in thick and heavy bands about her face.

"It feels odd, does it not, to be rid of that heavy hair," Amy said, reading her twin's feelings. "Makes you feel almost light-headed, doesn't it?"

Eve nodded. For a moment, and a moment only, she regretted her rashness in hacking away at her own glory. The hours spent in combing and brushing, in washing and dressing, styling and just simply playing with it all—

but she was not one for regrets. She hugged her sister. "No one could tell us apart," she said.

"I can," Miss Fisher said dryly.

"Well, Lord Barras certainly won't know the difference!" said Eve. "Oh, what will Thomas think when he sees? But of course by the time he and Papa return from abroad, we won't look like a pair of snake-headed creatures, for you know that is what Medusa was!"

"I don't think we look snake-headed at all," Amy said. "I think we look rather fashionable. Short hair is all the rage this year, according to *La Belle Assemblée*."

"Then we are finally all the rage," Eve said with a laugh. "Come, let us sweep up the carnage before one of the housemaids finds it and has a fit. Our story will simply be that I have returned to Italy as a slave of fashion, and instantly had to have an invalid's cut to be *à la mode*." Using the firebrush and shovel, she swept her shorn locks into the grate, trying not to feel a small pang of regret.

"And this will remain our little secret in this room, between the three of us," Eve commanded, setting a tinder so that the hair, together with several outdated issues of the *Edinburgh Review,* quickly disappeared into smoke curling up the chimney. "As much as I feel everyone here can be trusted, I think that they would play their parts better without having to act them out."

"There I must agree with you," Miss Fisher said. "This will remain between our confidences."

Replacing the fire tools by the grate, Eve stopped to peer again at her new reflection in the mantel mirror. "Yes, our little secret," she repeated, and frowned slightly at herself.

It would be better, she decided, if her other little secret remained known only to herself. A little act of twin deception was one thing, but she was certain that even

Amy would have been utterly and sincerely horrified if she knew what her twin's next mission in England was to be.

It was the first time in her life she had withheld something from Amy, but Eve knew that it would be better for both of them if her sister were left blissfully ignorant of coming events, even if that meant not being completely honest.

Eve pushed her hands through the new soft curls that framed her face, as if she could push the faint trace of uneasiness out of her mind.

Since she had been abroad, she had begun to realise that a secret only remained a secret if no one else knew about it.

Besides, she did so hate scenes, and she was utterly certain that her mission, had it become known, would have been the cause of a very grand one indeed, particularly if Aunt Seale had gotten wind of it.

Chapter
Three

"I REALLY CANNOT APPROVE of this, Miss Dartwood, it is simply not done," Mr. Shelldrake said for perhaps the tenth time, as he sat beside Eve in the dusty halls of Westerby's Auction Houses on the High in Oxford. On the podium, the auctioneer was knocking down an Egyptian mummy case, complete with mummy, for upwards of two hundred pounds.

Beneath her heavy veil, Eve bit her lip. She had discovered on the journey back from Naples that Mr. Shelldrake, like some wines, did not travel well. For six weeks, they had solidly grated upon each other's nerves. Mr. Shelldrake was of the opinion that the female sex was a frail and shrinking flower, inferior to the male sex both intellectually and physically. Eve, brought up to believe she could accomplish anything, had found his patronising attitude a sore trial.

And now, although she would have cheerfully allowed herself to be encased in that mummy case alive before admitting it, she very much feared that he had been correct; it was simply not done.

She was the only female present in the small and intense gathering today, and felt her presence to be distinctly unwelcome. The other bidders, almost all of them of a musty, scholarly mien, did not precisely stare her out of countenance, but she still felt their disapproval of her presence as if it were a palpable thing, and felt her bravado dimming considerably.

"I cannot imagine what Sir August had in mind when he commissioned you for this auction," Shelldrake said, sighing.

Eve, feeling the weight of the flat and disapproving stare of an elderly gentleman dusted with snuff seated to her left, was almost ready to agree, when the auctioneer's assistant brought forth the Etruscan goddess, holding it aloft so that she could be seen by the bidders.

The ambience, until this point, had been distinctly apathetic; one old collector, a well-known don at King's College, had drifted off to sleep, snoring softly.

But now there was a slight stir in the audience, and several heads turned, Eve's among them, as a stranger made a quiet entrance and took a seat in the gallery directly opposite Eve.

He was so different from the other gentlemen assembled there that even Eve had to study him out of the corner of her eye, interested to note that at the very least, they were the youngest people in attendance.

He was not precisely handsome; his features were far too craggy and strong for such a description, nor was he dressed in the first stare of elegance. His boots were caked with mud and his hair, of a fair color, was a disheveled clot of curls that obviously had missed the ministrations of his valet. He wore simple buckskin pantaloons and a carelessly knotted neckcloth. She could tell at a glance that he needed no assistance to shrug himself into his simple blue coat of bath superfine. Accustomed to the more dandified ways of the gentlemen of Naples, she dismissed him as of little interest until, happening to sense her eyes upon himself, he turned slightly in his seat. Lifting a quizzing glass to his eye, he proceeded to look her up and down in such a manner that she felt undressed, a twisted smile on his lips and a slight, almost mocking bow making her turn about and sit bolt upright, her ankles and knees firmly together. She was glad he could not see the flush that stole up her cheeks beneath the veil, and sorry he could not see the killing look she returned to him before giving all of her attention to the Etruscan goddess.

No more than a foot high, and made from terracotta, the goddess had long been a part of the late Sir Mortimer Justice's notable collection, and had long been coveted by Sir August as one of the most notable surviving examples of its culture unearthed for the modern world. Painted in polychrome, it had survived the ages remarkably well, and the lady's kohl-rimmed eyes still had a certain glint to them as she held out her twin serpents before her, her painted smile mischievous, her bright dress festive and, well, rather *risqué* with its exposed décolleté.

But Eve could see that once Sir August had beheld the little goddess, he would want her, for she was a wonderful piece, and quite rare, to have survived thousands of centuries buried in an Aegean tomb.

Nervously, she shifted in her seat as the auctioneer droned on about the goddess's provenance and dimensions, and announced that they would start the bidding at three hundred pounds.

Mr. Shelldrake's intake of breath was inaudible, but Eve felt it, and understood that this floor bid was higher than the cautious agent would have liked. Well did Sir Augustus understand his man; at that point Shelldrake, using his own judgement, would have withdrawn from the bidding entirely. A conservative and prudent man, he would have refused to risk his employer's capital upon such a venture. But Mr. Shelldrake did not have the heart and soul of a collector, as did Sir August, and when he had appointed his daughter to bid for him, he had impressed her deeply with his desire to add this single most precious specimen to his collection.

Eve took a deep breath and raised her paddle.

"Three-fifty," the auctioneer announced expressionlessly.

From across the room, an ancient parson in rusty black scratched his nose.

"Three seventy-five, gentlemen. Madam?"

Eve raised her paddle again.

"Four hundred," the auctioneer announced.

So far, the auction was proceeding to rule, and the don drifted back to sleep again.

"Four twenty-five," the auctioneer said, accepting a bid from the art dealer de Grace.

"Four-fifty," he called, accepting Eve's bid.

"Five hundred," said the blond man across the aisle lazily, and several gentlemen, astonished at the sound of a voice other than the auctioneer's, actually turned to stare.

But the carelessly dressed gentleman merely smiled,

leaning back in his chair and throwing one long and well-muscled leg over the other, his attitude one of boredom.

Eve shot him a furious look and raised her paddle. "Five twenty-five."

With a lazy smile in her direction, the young gentleman rubbed the side of his nose.

"Six hundred," the auctioneer said.

He had, Eve decided, the look of a Corinthian, a sporting gentleman. The nose that he rubbed had been broken, and while it did not detract from the masculinity of his features, it led her to believe that he was a practitioner of the horrid sport of boxing.

She waved her paddle.

"Six-fifty, to the lady," the auctioneer said, looking askance toward the gentleman.

No one else was bidding now but the two of them, and the audience was watching their competition with interest.

Lazily, the Corinthian waved long fingers in the air.

"Seven hundred to the gentleman."

"Miss Dartwood!" Shelldrake hissed, appalled.

But Eve, with the vision of Sir August's commission before her, was not to be dissuaded. She raised her hand, palm open.

"Eight hundred to the lady!" he called, entering into the spirit with unprofessional excitement. Doubtless, Westerby's, a most staid and conservative house, had never seen such excitement in all its hundred years of business. Several assistants in their livery had come to stand in the doorway to watch, as the Corinthian gentleman, with a look of extreme boredom, circled thumb and forefinger.

"Eight-fifty to the gentleman!"

There was a murmur through the crowd, and all

eyes were upon Eve as she bit her lower lip and plunged breathlessly onward. Angrily, she waved her paddle.

"Nine hundred pounds to the lady!"

The Corinthian turned and smiled at Eve. His look was so familiar, and so thoroughly amused that she yearned to deliver him a sharp setdown.

"One thousand to the gentleman!"

"Miss Dartwood!" Shelldrake hissed, laying a hand on her sleeve. "You must not! You cannot!"

"Watch me," Eve murmured, the fire of competition in her veins.

"Eleven hundred to the lady."

In no way distressed, the gentleman waved languidly.

"Twelve hundred to the gentleman."

"Miss Dart—"

Not to be outdone, Eve waved her paddle furiously.

"Thirteen hundred to the lady. Your bid, sir."

The Corinthian's eyes narrowed. Clearly, the spirit of battle was stirred in his blood also; but his signal, a mere nod of the head, was delivered almost casually.

"Fourteen hundred to the gentleman. Madam, your bid?"

"Fifteen hundred!" Eve cried.

"No more, absolutely no more, I beg of you, Miss Dartwood," Shelldrake implored her furiously. "Fifteen hundred is our entire budget for this year. Sir August cannot go over that."

Eve lowered her paddle, glowering furiously at the Corinthian beneath her veil, as if daring him to outbid her.

The smile he gave her was triumphant as he raised a single finger.

"Sixteen hundred to the gentleman. Madam, your bid?"

With a grand gesture, Eve rose and gathered her veil and her skirts about herself. She felt herself to be in the absolute right of things, and was only restrained from bidding higher by the absolute knowledge that fifteen hundred was the top price Sir August had instructed her to pay. She could not and would not go against her father's orders, but still, it galled her deeply to see the Etruscan goddess knocked down to this grinning sportsman.

"Let us leave, Shelldrake," she commanded, and heard him sigh with relief as he rose from his seat.

"To the gentleman for sixteen hundred," the auctioneer announced. "And if I may say so sir, an excellent choice."

As she was sailing majestically past, the gentleman gave her a bow from his seat. "Allow me to congratulate you upon your fine tastes, madam—and a most interesting contest," he said.

For once in her life entirely nonplussed, Eve could only sniff, in just the way that she had heard Aunt Seale sniff a hundred times, as she drew her skirts away and sailed past him, nose in the air.

"I wonder," she heard him say, "what secrets lie beneath that ugly veil."

"Odious" she hissed beneath her breath, but Shelldrake was already half dragging her out the door, relieved that the ordeal was over. In his mind, he had been proved entirely correct; women did not belong in auction houses.

Chapter Four

EVE'S TEMPER WAS FIERCE, but it flared and died with the speed of a rocket, and by the time she had returned to Dartwood House, instructed Jane to burn the hated veil, and changed into a cool dress of rose-sprigged muslin tied with a green sash, she was somewhat restored, even if still inclined to brood over her failure to Sir August.

Nonetheless, when she joined Amy and Miss Fisher in the gazebo for tea, she was still a little broody, causing her companions to exchange a look.

"So, did you accomplish all your shopping in Oxford?" Miss Fisher asked her, and had to ask her twice before Eve stirred herself to reply.

"What? Oh, no, that is, I found it all sadly depressing. The books I wanted were not in the library and they were all out of those two-and-six stockings at Mill-banke's," she said, spreading jam on a scone and feeling perfectly dreadful at having to deceive her sister and her former mentor so callously. Still, it was better than the shock and protest she would have received had she told them her real mission in town, she reflected, biting into her scone.

"Well, we have some fortunate news for you," Amy said, her eyes dancing. "We have just had word from Aunt Seale that she has encountered Lady Dolby and means to go on to London with her for a few days, so we are spared that, at least. I think she's getting new teeth," she added matter of factly.

"Good. Perhaps that will spare us the company of this Lord Barras person," Eve said around bites. She had not realised how very hungry she was, and now fell to with gusto. "Besides," she added, "It was so very hot in town that all I could think of was returning to the countryside."

"Well, I don't see why you had to wear that heavy pelisse, Eve," Amy remarked. "When you left, you looked as if you were going out into the arctic."

Eve bit her lip. Before she could make a reply, Tallant appeared from the rose path, looking somewhat distressed.

"Excuse me, Miss Eve, Miss Amy," he said unhappily, "but there is a Lord Barras who's come calling, for Miss Amy. I told him that the ladies were not at home to visitors, but he was *quite* insistent."

Amy's nerveless fingers dropped the Meissen teacup she held in her hand, and it rolled across the cover, its delicate bowl shattering.

"Oh," she said, and in the confusion of mopping up and rescuing pastries from the disaster, Eve, whose frustration had found an unexpected ventilation, said to Tallant, "Tell Lord Barras I shall be right there, please."

To her great relief, Tallant merely nodded. "Very good, Miss Amy," he said. "I shall attend to this—"

"No, no, please, send out one of the footmen and go and announce me to Lord Barras, please," Eve instructed, delighted that even the butler could not tell her from her sister in a moment of confusion.

"Oh, Eve, you cannot! You must not!" Amy pleaded after he had gone, while Miss Fisher tsked and sopped up spilled tea.

"I can and I will!" Eve hissed, throwing down her napkin and rising from the table. "Now remember, you are me and I am you, and I will be rid of the odious man as soon as possible! Believe me, I am spoiling to be as unpleasant to someone as possible today, and I should hate to take it out on the innocent!"

"Eve!" Miss Fisher said sharply, but Miss Dartwood was already on her way into the house, leaving her sister and Miss Fisher to soothe each other.

Eve was absolutely certain that it would take no acting ability whatsoever to thoroughly and firmly depress the pretensions of an unwelcome, unexpected and unwanted visitor. If Lord Barras thought for one moment that he could sweep into a lady's house, intimidate the servants and *demand* to see a hostess who was indisposed then he must be an opponent worthy of her mettle!

"Broke to bridle indeed," she murmured to herself as she swept down the long hallway toward the green salon where Tallant customarily left visitors cooling their heels. Fire and ice snapped from her green eyes, and she put a hand to her newly shortened hair as she sailed through the high portals into the eau-de-nil room.

The tart Sally that had been on the tip of her tongue

was suddenly lost there as she beheld the man who stood, his back toward her, looking up at a fragment of a Doric pediment on a pedestal beside the fireplace.

At first, she thought her senses were deceiving her, but, sensing her presence, the man turned, one eyebrow cocked, and she knew that fate had played an outrageous trick upon her.

"*You!*" she exclaimed.

The Corinthian's twisted smile transformed his face as he made a bow. "Miss Dartwood," he said calmly, lifting his quizzing glass to his eye. "How very much in looks you are today! Evidently this spell of fine weather we have been enjoying has done your health some good."

Eve was rarely nonplussed, but she found herself opening and closing her mouth without any sound emerging from her lips. Not only was my lord Barras the very same man who had outbid her that morning at Westerby's, he had not bothered to change from his mud-splattered boots and his careless neckcloth to come a-courting.

Eve's eyes narrowed slightly. If her sister had been moonstruck mad for the man, she still would have moved heaven and earth to prevent the match.

Before she could protest, he had seated himself in a William Kent chair, as much at his ease as if he had been expected. "I have often heard about your father's fine collection of antiquities," he drawled, "and I must say, so far I am not overly disappointed, although I am certain that that jasper goblet on yon table is a recent forgery. Damned clever forgers, those Romans. You must watch yourself from fore and aft when dealing with a broker from the Spanish Steps, you know!" Again, he smiled, his dark eyes hooded and amused.

Distracted, Eve picked up the goblet in question.

"Sir, this is fifth century and completely authentic! As you can see, it bears a medallion of the Emperor Tiberius on one side."

Lazily, he waved it away. "I might have made the same mistake when d'Ursini offered me the pair, but I happily recalled Tiberius's birth was sixty years later than the classical rage for vessels carved from precious metals. By then, as you know, Suetonious informs us that the jasper mines had been long closed. The barbarian hoardes had overrun Turkey."

Eve, who knew no such thing, nonetheless felt a strong urge to hurl the heavy wine goblet at Barras's handsome blond head.

Instead, she carefully replaced the object on the table among its other antique companions and stood over him in her most imposing manner.

"And to what do we owe this unexpected visit? Tallant informs me that you were told we were not at home, sir, and yet you insisted upon gaining entrance."

"Yes, I did, didn't I?" he said, smiling. "I am a rather forceful person, you know."

"I fail to see that bad manners should be a cause for self-congratulation."

"Ho! Away from your aunt, you do have a tongue in your head, do you not, Miss Dartwood?" Clearly amused, he continued to smile at her from beneath those heavy eyelids, making himself very much at home.

Eve, recalling that she was supposed to be Amy, merely nodded. "I think," she said coldly, "that you will find that I am not at all who you believed me to be when we met in Bath." That much was true, she told herself sternly.

"Indeed," he returned agreeably, thrusting his long

legs out before him. "It is refreshing to see that you are not as namby-pamby as I had believed, Miss Dartwood."

"I should hope not. Indeed, you will find that as I recovered my health, I also recovered my spirit! Now, what may I do for you, my lord? As Tallant told you, we are not at home to callers today. My—my sister has lately returned from Naples, you see, and the journey has fatigued her considerably."

"Naples, yes, I believe you mentioned your twin was abroad with your father. I must meet her, of course, but not at once. She sounds devilish like a hoyden and that is one thing I cannot bear."

"Really," Eve said in ice-water tones.

"Oh, yes. Your aunt tells me that she is a regular devil in skirts," Barras continued. "But then, most educated women are! You have proved to be a notable exception, and for that reason, if no other, I am grateful."

"I am so pleased," Eve replied dryly.

"Oh, I am sure we shall manage to scrape together somehow. After all, I am famous for my ability to charm anyone."

"So I see. You have certainly charmed me into a stupor. So, if you will please state your business, I will then go upstairs and have an attack of the vapours. Brought on, of course, by your fatal charms."

Somehow or another, Eve felt as if the tone of the conversation had been removed from her control and allowed, through some mysterious means, to slide into utter nonsense. Under any other circumstances, she would have been diverted. But, as things stood, she was in no mood to allow this man to amuse her.

He was shaking his head and smiling. "Well, if you must know, I happened to be in the neighbourhood and thought I might pay a call upon you. You see, I came up from London to attend an auction at Westerby's—I rode horseback all the way, hence I appear in all my dirt, but you see, sometimes I prefer to travel without my man and my groom. So much easier that way."

"Without seeing your horse, I can make no comment upon the wisdom of your travelling without your groom, but I think you really must miss your valet," Eve snipped.

But Barras seemed impervious. Rather than the insulted reaction she had hoped for, he merely smiled again and shrugged his shoulders. "I am certain that he would agree with you, for all of his attempts to turn me into a man of fashion have been notably unsuccessful, and are a sad source of frustration to him. My friend Brummel says that his genius is sadly wasted upon me, and that I am a hopeless poltroon in matters of sartorial display. And I daresay Brummel is correct. However, it don't signify."

"I suppose I am to be impressed with your friendship with the famous Beau Brummel," Eve's tone was acid.

His look was slightly startled. "No! Please! I beg you not to think that I am a name-dropper. That at least is not one of my faults, although driving people mad may supplant it."

"Indeed, sir." Eve almost smiled at his wit.

"No, no! The fact of the matter was that I only heard this morning that the Justice estate was auctioning off the old boy's Etruscan goddess, and that was a piece I have always coveted for my own collections. So, in order to save time, I took off from the Albany this morning on horseback and left my valet and my groom to follow with all the appropriate state."

"I see," Eve replied dangerously. "You must have ridden like the wind."

"Oh, I'm a bruising rider," Barras replied cheerfully and without any false modesty. "But you know, the oddest things will happen, and one of them happened to me today. I daresay it shall take me weeks to recover from the shock."

"Oh, and what was that?"

Barras shook his head. "I was almost outbid by a female! Can you imagine such a thing?"

"No, never," Eve replied, straight-faced and rigid.

Barras shook his head. "Well, it almost happened. She could have beaten me out, too, for the bidding climbed to sixteen hundred pounds, and I was not prepared to go any higher than that. In fact, I was prepared to be a gentleman and let her have the thing, but she dropped out at fifteen hundred. I felt sorry for her."

"Perhaps fifteen hundred was all she had," Eve replied, utterly fascinated.

"Perhaps so. But you know, I felt sorry for her! Never before in my life have I felt sorry for someone I've bid against, but she was wearing the ugliest veil, as thick as a tea cover, and I thought to myself, well, any female who has to wear a veil that thick must be dashed ugly and need a bit of beauty in her life, so why not let her have it?"

Behind her back, Eve's fingers clenched and unclenched. "Oh, I don't know," she said in a strangled voice. "Perhaps she was hiding a great beauty from the stares of so many men!"

Barras shook his head and rose to his feet. "Well, I am sure I don't know, but I'll tell you, I'd wager yon little goddess herself that she was as ugly as sin, poor thing, to be draped like a funeral cortege."

Before Eve could reply, he had taken her hand and shaken it. "Well, I must make my leave! I'm putting up at

Lady Seale's, and she informed me before she left London that she would be delayed for a day or two with her dressmaker, so I suppose I am to be left to my own devices."

"I am certain you will contrive something to amuse yourself." Eve was almost trembling with indignation, but she managed to conceal it.

"I am certain that I will! Shall we plan to go riding tomorrow morning? I'll come by for you in my phaeton after breakfast."

"I—I—"

"Good, that's settled then. Well, I do look forward to meeting your sister. Good day, Miss Dartwood."

And with that, he was out the door.

Eve, pushed beyond all bearing, picked up the jasper goblet and hurled it after his departing head. It smashed into the wall and shattered into a thousand pieces.

"Ugly!" she hissed, but Lord Barras, returning to inspect the damage, merely clucked his tongue.

"Really, Miss Dartwood, you must not be so clumsy! But you *do* see what I mean, do you not?" He bent and picked up a fragment of the goblet. "Glass, not jasper. Jasper would never shatter in that fashion. Good day."

"Oh! Odious, odious man!" Eve hissed as his hoofbeats receded down the driveway. "I'll show you yet!" she swore in a rare ginger-headed rage.

Chapter
Five

LORD BARRAS WAS AS good as his word; at half after nine, he appeared in the driveway, his groom behind him, driving a handsome yellow-wheeled high-perch phaeton drawn by a high-stepping team of four matched bays. There was, at least, nothing careless in his turnout, for it would have been hard to find a better-groomed team or a more gleaming vehicle.

With Amy's "do be careful, do," echoing in her ears, Eve stepped out of the house, still drawing on her gloves. The biting greeting that had been upon the tip of her tongue wavered when she saw Barras's equipage, for she was no mean judge of horseflesh herself, and knew quality when she saw it.

Happily for my lord, his valet had arrived at Seale

Abbey together with his groom, and his attire was far neater than it had been the previous day, although still lacking in the fads and foibles of sartorial display that would have qualified him to sit among men of fashion. His boots were polished, although not to a looking-glass shine, his buckskin breeches brushed, but not embarrassingly tight to his neat figure, and his driving coat bespoke the simplicity of Scott rather than the dandified fripperies of Nugee. About his neck he had knotted a spotted kerchief that proclaimed him a member of the Four Horse Club, but his shirt points remained almost unfashionably low, so that he was able to turn his head about from one side to the other without wilting them.

Today, Eve was able to see that he was not at all an unhandsome man, although lacking in the collie-dog bones that some would have considered the hallmark of good breeding. A little above the medium height, he was not, she noted, an ill-made man; although he was inclined toward stockiness, rather than the lissome thinness of, say, Thomas Perry. But then, what man could possibly match her handsome Thomas, so sensitive, so poetic? Certainly not this oaf, for whom the romantic and the otherworldly were doubtless scornful vices. In fact, nothing could have been more worldly than the manner in which he surveyed her, from the top of her straw coal-scuttle bonnet to the tips of her orange nankeen boots, a look that made her feel as if she were in her shift.

"If," she announced without preamble, "you intend to lift that odious quizzing glass to your eye and look me up and down as if I were a horse at Tattersall's as you did—*that is*, as some men do, then I shall scream."

Barras, however, merely smiled and gave her one of his mocking bows, in no way discomfited. "As you can see, I have left my quizzing glass in the care of my valet.

And, Miss Dartwood, I was about to say that I thought you look charming today. Carriage dress from Paris? I thought I recognised the style—even Bonaparte's parvenu pretensions cannot quite depress that essential European look. A most excellent colour for you, also. Pomona green? Or is that eau de nil?"

"Italian actually, from Naples. I—that is, my sister bought it for me there," Eve replied, almost meekly. She could see the humour dancing in his dark eyes and yearned to smile, but dared not, lest she break character. With some effort she set her features into a look of haughty unpleasantness as she allowed him to hand her up into the swaying perch of the phaeton.

Barras's groom, with a shake of his head, made for the Dartwood stables in hopes of more congenial company than that provided by this ginger-haired hellion. A high-perch phaeton seated only two; there was no trap for a groom.

Eve very much wanted to compliment Barras on his horses and vehicle, as much because she ached to have a turn at the reins as because she appreciated his style, but she contented herself with watching in grudging admiration as he took the reins in his hands and started down the drive at a spanking pace, clearing the narrow brick pillars with only inches to spare.

"So how do you come to know so much about ladies' fashions?" she asked.

Barras shook his head. "The proper answer would be that I have sisters, would it not?" he asked, unperturbed. "But the truth of the matter is that I stand upon very good terms with certain females of expensive and knowledgeable taste in clothing, if not suitors."

This time, Eve had to laugh; her sense of humour, never too far from the surface, was tickled by this outrageous statement. "If you mean that you keep a mistress, then say so! You cannot shock me with such fustian, sir!"

"That is a great pity, for I meant to do so," he replied equably. "After all, a man's mistresses should be of great interest to his future wife."

"But I am not your future wife yet, nor am I totally certain that I want to be. A female, after all, can change her mind."

"Ho! Merely because a man has kept a mistress before his marriage?"

"Do not expect missish behaviour from me, my lord! You may find yourself at a standstill," Eve warned him lightly. "Besides, what if you should choose to continue to see your light-o'-love *after* marriage?"

"Then I should expect my wife to turn a blind eye, just as I should do if she chose another interest. After the heir, of course," he said blandly.

It was too much for Eve; she gave a little gurgle of laughter and shook her head. "At least you are frank!" she managed to exclaim as the countryside bore away beneath them.

"I am never anything but frank, Miss Dartwood. I find roundaboutation suits me very ill. Fancified phrases and all the stuff-and-nonsense of romance are such tripe as I find a dead bore."

"A strange wooing indeed," Eve replied. "Your mistresses must find you an odd sort of creature."

"Mist*ress*. One, and one only. And since ours is a business transaction, and she is the most pragmatic of females, we deal together very well. Her name is Mrs. Fotherby."

Eve could not quite peer about her coal-scuttle bonnet to see his face, but she bit her lip and frowned, for some reason out of sorts with this unknown Mrs. Fotherby. The daughter of a widower, she of course had no illusions about the human passions, but could not resist pursuing the subject, if only to tease a little.

"Mrs. Fotherby must be a rather tough nut," she ventured.

"On the contrary, she is the most feminine and complaisant of creatures," Barras returned, unruffled.

"And the most venial and impatient, too, I should imagine."

"She is a vision of loveliness, and her demands are not excessive. Frequently I have had to press small gifts into her hands."

"A paragon of all virtue! I am surprised you do not marry her!"

"I would, but Mrs. Fotherby is married to Mr. Fotherby, you see."

Eve did see, or thought that she did, but what she did not see was the smile that played about Barras's countenance.

"I see!" she said at last, her feathers ruffled. Inside the brim of her bonnet, she bit her lip. Thomas would never have a mistress, she thought, and if he did, he would never ever discuss her with the woman he was courting. Poor Amy! No wonder she had been in such a quake! No, this Barras would never do for her shy and retiring sister, not at all. Mistresses!

She opened up a second front. "Of course, you know, if you continue to see Mrs. Fotherby, and we are married, I shall be forced to seek consolation elsewhere."

"Oh, of course! As soon as we have the heir, of course, you are free to do as you wish," he said, in no way shocked. "I am certain that there are any number of gentlemen who find red hair most attractive!"

"And I assure you, sir, that there are!" Eve snapped.

"Mrs. Fotherby is a raven-haired brunette," he continued thoughtfully, adding quickly, "and Mr. Fotherby is bald, so don't ask me what colour his hair is."

Eve felt quite dizzy with this conversation. She suspected that Lord Barras was teasing her in a most tongue-in-cheek manner, and turned to look at him, but the face he presented to her was bland; she did not detect the glitter in his eye. Odious, odious, odious! she thought, but aloud she merely repeated, "Of course, while you are with Mrs. Fotherby, I shall seek Consolation elsewhere." She wanted very much to shock him with blue conversation. "Perhaps a handsome half-pay hussar. And of course, I shall need to make him little gifts appropriate to his station in my life."

Eve had learned a great deal about the ways of the world while in Naples.

"I quite understand, and I am sure that you will be able to provide for him from your allowance."

"That is another matter. I have a great fancy to be *very* fashionable, you know, to become all the rage in London. I happen to adore balls and parties and routs and an endless whirl of Society. As Lady Barras, I intend to go everywhere and do everything, and I shall of course, need your escort, so it will doubtless cut into your time with your antiquities, and you will of course, be prepared for that? And opera," Eve added with diabolical inspiration. "I adore opera, you know, could go every night." No gentleman of her acquaintance, not even Thomas, liked opera. That should surely stick in his craw, she thought.

He whistled a few bars from *The Magic Flute*.

"We shall have a box," he promised.

"And the *vernissages* at the Royal Academy, of course. And I *will* have my portrait done by Reynolds and Romney and Sir Thomas. It is a great deal too bad that

Mr. Gainsborough is dead, for I should wish my likeness taken by him, also."

"They shall hang proudly in the gallery at Highgrove."

"That is another thing. I understand Highgrove is Tudor, and I am certain that it must be dreadfully dusty, and that your chimneys smoke, and everything is terribly old-fashioned." There, she thought, dig at him about his beloved Highgrove. He may put you down in the middle of the Oxford Road, but at least he will be out of Amy's life—and yours—forever. "As Lady Barras, I will of course want everything done over, and some lovely modern furniture from Bullock's installed. And," she added, horribly inspired, "I have a great fancy for *chinoiserie,* just like the Regent has at Carleton House, so we shall have a great deal of that, if you please."

"Just as you like," he replied, unperturbed, and again, Eve tried to peer around the brim of her bonnet to see his expression; she was rewarded with a bland smile.

She drew in her breath and closed her eyes, frustrated. Was there no end to this man's enraging complaisance? She would have preferred an adversary worthy of her worst, rather than one who listened impassively to all she had to say.

"Of course, I have a great fancy to be a viscountess," she ventured airily. "I trust that your family has a suitable collection of jewels?"

"Oh yes, I can recall 'em on m'mother. Great set of emeralds, some sapphire pieces, a ruby parure, and of course there's the Barras diamonds, but they were grand, too grand for my mother, used to say her head and her back always ached whenever she had to wear 'em for state events."

"I suppose they will do, but I should also like to go to Rundell and Bridge myself and select the pieces that will be mine, you know, rather than the family's. I," she said firmly, smoothing out her gloves, "have a great fancy for pearls and emeralds together, huge pearls and emeralds, nothing tiny and insignificant, but as big as birds' eggs. Nothing else will do."

"Messrs. Rundell and Bridge are excellent jewellers, and I am certain that they will be able to fulfill your needs."

"And huge rubies, of course. The biggest they can find. I must have a great deal of jewellery, you know, to look the part of a fashionable viscountess."

She hoped he would have apoplexy at her vulgarity, but he merely reined in his team to an inch, allowing a dray cart to pass them on the opposite side of the road.

Eve admired his skill, but said nothing for several miles, busily wracking her brain for further examples of her—or, strictly, Amy's—unsuitability as a prospective Lady Barras.

"I despise antiques, you know. You cannot imagine how dreadful it is to grow up in a house where one can barely move for all the nasty marble bits and pieces of other people's anatomy strewn about as if it were something attractive. You shall have to house your collection elsewhere."

"I shall build a Chinese wing in which to display it," he promised, and whistled a bit more Mozart between his teeth. "If it's Bullock and *chinoiserie* you want, then you shall have it."

The day was becoming warm; behind the hedgerows, the open fields stretched over the rolling hills, as neat and bordered as a patchwork quilt of green, gold, and brown. Here and there, spring flowers lifted their heads toward the sunshine in the delicate pastels of the season. A flight of starlings took from the blooming hedgerows to the sky, and the smell of rich earth filled the air as teams of ploughmen broke the earth for late crops of late wheat and barley. Not for the first time since her return from Naples, Eve felt her very English soul stir within her, and if she could, she would have embraced the world she had known since birth with renewed love. At once, she yearned to express these feelings to her companion, and again, was forced to restrain herself, reminding herself that she was Amy, not Eve.

Truly, this playacting *was* trying. Never again would she doubt the talents of Mrs. Siddons; she felt a positive admiration for that lady's work on the stage.

"As my viscountess, of course, you should expect every gratification. I would not be a Barras if I did not say so, for the Barrases, you know, are always good to their women."

"At least in the material sense," Eve replied. How she yearned to drop this pretense and beg him to hand her the reins! "Of course, I shall expect all of my clothes to come from Paris, and we shall travel abroad a great deal, now that the peace has been established. But no ruins, I beg of you! So very dull! My sister might find them interesting, but I find antiquities a dead bore. I intend to spend all of my time going to the fashionable ton parties and buying new clothes. Hideously expensive clothes! I intend to spend four or five hundred pounds at a clip! I will not wear a gown more than once, you know. And a French maid! I must have a French maid! Of course, a good French maid is worth her weight in gold, and quite thirty or forty pounds a year, but I must have one."

"Of course. I would not deny you that."

"I should hope not! After all, I intend to become the most fashionable female in all of London, and that takes a great deal of time and money! Why, you would be amazed at the amount of time I spend each morning in front of the mirror just getting ready to come down to breakfast!"

"Just so!" Lord Barras said.

"And horses! I must have my own team and a phaeton and two or three hacks in town to ride in the park at the fashionable hour. And a barouche for calling, and a carriage, of course, with an *enormous* crest on the door so that everyone should know I am a viscountess. And of course, I shall need a string of hunters! I assume that in addition to your seat, we shall have a box at Melton, and a lodge in Scotland? I have a fancy to hunt and to shoot."

"I thought you did not like horses."

"A lady can change her mind," Eve replied far more blithely than she was feeling. Amy, of course, was less than fond of horses, she reminded herself sternly.

Inspiration seized her and she said quickly, "Did I tell you that I adore playing cards? None of this silver-loo or whist, either, but deep basset and faro are my games. I suppose Aunt Seale did not tell you that I lost oh, quite five hundred pounds at faro in London, did she? I thought not."

"Then we must play sometime. I consider myself no mean gamester." Clearly, this was not the rout she had hoped it would be, and Eve bit her lip, considering her options, of which she seemed to be running quite dry.

At that point, there was the sound of the horn on the road ahead, and the distant rumble and jingle of a massive coach.

"That," Eve remarked absently, "will be the Northern Flyer Coach. Drat the luck, we shall be stuck behind it until we get to Five Points!"

Even as she spoke, they were drawing up fast behind the lumbering mail coach. Laden with passengers, boxes, and several crates of squawking chickens, the red-and-gold coach, drawn by a team of six heavy horses, moved with almost stately majesty up the narrow road.

Lord Barras slackened the ribbons in his hands and his horses picked up speed.

"You wouldn't!" Eve protested. "You can't! See, there is a farm cart bearing down on us from the other side of the road! Barras!"

But she spoke too late, for he was whipping the phaeton around the coach and directly into the path of the uncoming cart, not more than twenty feet away.

They passed the coach so closely that Eve could see the open mouths and white eyes of the passengers on the roof as they went past.

With barely inches to spare, they pulled in before the coach, just as the farm cart lumbered past.

"Oh, you are a fool! We could have been killed, or at the very least overturned."

The face Barras turned toward her was bland. "But we were not, were we?" he asked. "I am nothing, ma'am, but a credible whip!"

"A foolish whip! A mere whipster!" Eve exclaimed, truly vexed as she adjusted her bonnet and pulled her skirts together about her ankles.

"Could you do better? You speak of wanting your own horses and phaetons and teams—"

Stung, Eve reached over and removed the ribbons from his hands. "I shall show you!" she exclaimed, and whipped the team up to a brisk trot.

"Very well, then! Show me!" Barras commanded, his eyes narrowed as she set the phaeton to the road, giving the horses their head until they were into a gallop.

They were approaching a bridge over a small brooklet, no more than a wooden pier wide enough to accommodate a single vehicle, if it travelled slowly and cautiously across the ancient planks.

Sir August would have been horrified to see his daughter approach this hurdle at a neck-or-nothing speed; but for some reason it was of Aunt Seale's horrified face that Eve thought as she guided the leader into the narrow dock. As the horses galloped over the creek, the entire structure shook in an ominous fashion, and she could feel through the reins that the high-strung and sensitive team would have shied away from a less steady and certain hand. But still, she did not breathe until the last hoof had again hit upon good firm earth. Then, she slowed the team gradually into a walk before handing the ribbons back to Barras.

"Not bad," he admitted. "On the whole, not bad at all. A bit ham-handed, but still, not bad at all."

"Ham-handed? *Ham-handed?*" Eve demanded, incensed. "Sir, I have never been ham-handed in my life!"

"A little practice would not come amiss. I shall be honoured to teach you a lighter touch, but not, I think, today. My groom would give me a proper dressing down if I brought my horses back too exhausted to eat their gruel. At any rate, I feel as if we have reached a most wonderful understanding, and I shall look forward to pursuing it tomorrow. Shall we say about the same time? And, if it is not a great deal of trouble, I think you might allow me to stay to lunch and see your father's collections."

"Doing it a bit too brown, sir!" Eve replied with spirit.

Barras inclined his head gravely. "I am only following your lead, ma'am," he said calmly. "You seem to appreciate the forthright."

"Oh, very well, then!" Eve knew when she had been bested at her own game, and grudgingly felt a sense of admiration for Lord Barras's sheer nerve. "Tomorrow, then!"

Chapter
Six

"ODIOUS, ODIOUS, ODIOUS MAN!" Eve brooded.

The evening was lovely, contrasting pale and dark in sapphire shades and delicate hues of celestial blue that stole in long summer shadows over the glories of the garden. The faint, sad-sweet potpourri of the Malmaison roses drifted on the gentle air, and a nightingale pitched its beautiful song from a larch tree nearby.

"You've been saying that ever since teatime," Amy pointed out gently. "Odious, odious, odious, over and over again." She plucked out a bit of a tune on her little tenor guitar, and bending her head, adjusted a key a quarter-tone upwards, strumming a clear chord. "Better," she murmured to herself.

Eve sipped at the last glass of her dinner wine and

leaned back in her seat. Tonight, in the twilight, dressed in white muslin, they looked more alike than ever, each one so fair and so red-haired. The copy of *La Belle Assemblée* she had been restlessly perusing lay on the Chippendale bench beside her, thrown carelessly down. As she stared moodily off into the fields beyond the garden, she felt a vague twinge of boredom. If she were still in Naples, she would be at the opera, or dancing at someone's ball, or lingering over the dinner table, engaged in passionate conversation with her dinner companions. Here, nothing had changed; Dartwood House moved on its own stately rhythms. It was rural, quiet, and infinitely a place of females, of secluded rustic comfort. And while she had missed it when she was in Naples, she had also become aware of another life, a life that was neither cloistered nor contemplative, but steadily and constantly changing, always stimulating, always active. She had grown to enjoy that life, and now, like a soldier retired from the wars, yearned for battle again.

"Odious man," she repeated thoughtfully, and wondered why Gervase Barras piqued her so.

Amy, oblivious, picked out a country air on her guitar, her long lissome fingers darting expertly and easily over the strings. This sort of life, Eve reflected, suited her sister very well, with her infinite capacity to keep herself busy and happily occupied with a variety of interests. Her gardening, her music, her reading, her needlework, her domestic concerns—all of these things filled Amy's life richly. Her idea of a happy evening was dining with neighbours and ancient friends from childhood, followed perhaps by some music or some tame parlour games: racing demon, snakes and ladders and, more daringly, perhaps a rubber or two of whist for penny stakes or fabulous, imaginary sums.

And Eve did not begrudge her that. Quietude was a part of Amy's character; in church, it had always been Eve who had been roundly castigated for squirming in her seat and looking about her, half fatigued with the boredom of one of the vicar's interminable sermons, while Amy had sat quite still, and had even, wondrously, been able to discuss it all afterward at lunch.

In Naples, Eve had discovered her own natural inclinations toward the active. She had never felt so alive as she had among all the excitements to be found in the world, and she had been quite correct when she had told Barras that she enjoyed being fashionable, and going to parties and balls, that she liked to hunt and ride and pursue a life that was always in motion. In essence, the portrait she had painted of herself was a grotesque parody of reality—although she hoped she was not as *venial* as all of that!

"I was perfectly dreadful," she confessed moodily to her twin. "I was by turns vulgar, improper, greedy and just plain rude! And still, nothing could shock him! It was as if it didn't signify at all! And then, to top it all off, I took the ribbons from him and led his team, at close gallop, over the narrow little bridge on the creek! At a gallop! I was terribly afraid that I'd upset us, or hurt the horses! I wish you could have seen his team! All high steppers and all matched perfectly, not a rum fundy in the bunch! Whatever else he has, he's an excellent judge of horseflesh." Restlessly, she turned on the cushioned seat and threw her head back to the open face of the moon. "In Naples, the *Lazzaroni*, you know, still believe in the ancient lunar goddesses. You're supposed to make a wish the first night you see the full moon, and it will come true."

"Then I should wish for—I know not what," Amy said thoughtfully, her fingers plucking out an ancient folk song, full of longing. "Not for Lord Barras, certainly, but for someone who is kind, and gentle and understanding."

"Dull qualities indeed," Eve said with a sigh. "I should wish for someone who is bold and adventurous and—and a bit of a swashbuckler, who would sweep me away into a great many romantic adventures."

"But you have Thomas Perry, the poet," Amy pointed out.

"What? Oh yes, Thomas. Of course," Eve murmured vaguely. She felt a stab of guilt that he had not been more on her mind in recent times, but truth to tell, other things, most notably this disturbing Lord Barras, had preoccupied her. If she were very honest with herself, which she was not prepared to be at that moment, she would have admitted that she had not given much thought to her Italian romance since she had departed from Naples.

"Odious, odious man!" she said, sighing again, almost as if she could blame Lord Barras for this, also. She picked up *La Belle Assemblée* and flipped through the pages again before tossing it down on the cushions. "And tomorrow, again, I have to see him! He wants a tour of Papa's collection! Amy, never, ever, say that I never did anything for you."

"Why would I ever say that? You know how very grateful I am!" Amy cried, much wounded at such an accusation. "You are handling it all ever so much better than I could! Dearest Eve, could you—do you think that I am an ungrateful wretch? Oh, please, say it is not so!"

Amy put down her guitar and rose. On light and graceful feet, she threw herself upon her sister's shoulder. "Poor dear! Does it all seem terribly vexatious to you? I did not mean it to be so!"

Eve hugged her sister, and again felt the new distance between them, faint as a whisper. "No, no, no! You must never think such a thing!" she exclaimed fiercely. "Dearest, dearest Amy, we are sisters; I would do anything for you. It is just that I am so restless tonight. I yearn for a dance or a party or something—anything that is not dull and domestic!" She shook her head at her sister's expression.

"I don't understand what you mean," Amy said. "Why, Dartwood House is the best place in all the world!"

"No, I used to think so, but now I do not—there is a whole world out there, and I die to see it all! Naples, you know, was so different and exciting and—" before she could say it aloud, she stopped herself. And, she was going to say, I was simply Evelina Dartwood, not one of the Dartwood twins. She knew that sensitive Amy would take this in the wrong spirit, and try as Eve might, this was not a feeling that she could easily explain, even to herself. All of her life, she had been a part of a whole, and in the past eighteen months of being separated from her twin, she had reveled in the idea of being one single person, a unique identity. Surely, she thought, while she was gone, Amy must have felt this too?

No, she thought, looking into her sister's eyes, Amy had not felt it. Or leastways, not to express it.

She drew her sister to her and kissed her cheek gently. "Dear one, I am impossible! If I do not watch myself, I shall become the unpleasant person I am playing with Lord Barras, and make life utterly miserable for all of us—you, Tabby and me! Best I should take myself off to bed! I am fatigued from so much travelling, I think—it takes time to recover from these things. I will take myself off, and after a night's sleep I shall be as right as a trivet, never you worry!"

So saying, she slipped into the house, leaving Amy alone with her thoughts.

In her own way, Amy too, had been well aware of the

difference between her life as a twin and her life as a singleton, and while she was not as studied as her sister on the matter, she also felt their separation had changed her. While she loved Eve deeply, she had enjoyed being a whole person in her own right, and save for the matter of Lord Barras, had very much enjoyed her life in the past eighteen months without her sister's shadow.

Thoughtfully, she picked up her tenor guitar again, and placed her fingers on the fretboard. Without even thinking about it, she began to pick out an old French tune about love and yearning, a little hymn to the moonlight.

Behind her, a white marble statue of Diana, thousands of years old, gleamed in the pale light of the moon, and Amy turned to look at it, as if half expecting the ancient goddess to grant her deepest wish.

How much she yearned for love!

Amy bent forward over the box of the guitar and then threw her head back. In a light, lilting voice, she began to sing, so shyly and softly that no one in the house could have heard her.

"Où est mon amour?" she sang, and closed her eyes.

It may have been a trick of the moonlight and the shadow, but it seemed to the young man, who had walked up the driveway on silent feet and had stolen through the heavy June roses in search of the musician, that the statue of Diana winked at him as he came around the corner from the trellises.

This he considered to be a happy omen, and without so much as a word, he stole up on the slight, ginger-haired figure in white.

So silently did he move, and so engrossed was she in her music, that she did not even sense his presence until he had leaned down, put his arms about her and placed a kiss upon her open mouth.

Virginal though she might have been, Amy's first thoughts as she opened her eyes and beheld a handsome stranger's face so close to her own were not as horrific as might have been expected. The sensation of his lips against her own was quite pleasant, much more so than the rough wooing of the only other man who had ever tried to kiss her, my lord Barras, and the way in which this stranger's strong arms enveloped her gave her no cause for dread, but rather released an entirely new and entirely pleasant feeling within herself that she had never known before.

It was only when he moved back a few inches and looked at her that she felt a rosy flush stealing into her cheeks. He *was* handsome; of that there could be no doubt at all, for across a broad and marble forehead fell a mass of blue-black hair, framing a pair of ice-blue eyes surrounded by incredibly long black lashes, so lush and thick she had to resist an impulse to touch them with wondering fingertips. His bones were fine and delicate, his expression so ardent and adoring that she knew no fear, only a consuming sense that he was the most attractive man she had ever seen in her life.

Rather breathlessly, she noted the clean smell of his cologne and the niceness of his cravat and coat, an elegantly tailored bath superfine. In this, too, he compared favourably with Lord Barras's carelessness in dress.

In a happy daze, Amy took all of these small details in, without really feeling any great alarm, but an almost overwhelming sense of pleasure, as if strange, handsome, young men appeared in the garden at the drop of a wish.

"Dearest, dearest Eve!" he exclaimed, and broke the spell.

"But I am not Eve! I am her sister, Amy!" Her cheeks flamed as she pressed her hands against them. "You must be Thomas Perry! Oh, what must you think of me?"

Chapter
Seven

    "ON THE CONTRARY, WHAT must you think of *me*?" Thomas Perry asked in anguished tones. "Eve told me that she had a twin, but I never thought, never suspected—it must be a trick of the moonlight, but you are she—that is to say, I thought you were she! Miss—Amy! Miss Amy, there is *nothing* I can say or do to make you forgive me for the way in which I behaved—" His pale blue eyes bored into her gaze, imploring her. "You see, I thought to surprise Eve, and when I saw you sitting alone in the garden, I thought you were she and—and, well!"

    "Oh, yes, I do see, and you must not think anything of it! It—it seems a natural mistake. You see, we look so much alike that *everyone* mistakes us for each other—"

    "But you are not at all alike, now that I truly look

upon you," Thomas Perry said. "You have a certain delicacy that Eve does not have, for she is much more robust, you know. Indeed, you are much more—but I am mortified, and do not know what I can do to—" Confused, he broke off, and for a long moment, they simply stared into each other's eyes, as if hypnotized.

For a long moment, it was as if the rest of the world did not exist, and whole volumes of words were communicated in that single, lingering glance.

It was only when a light flickered in the house and a window was raised, the sound as loud as an explosion in the silence, that they realised that Thomas Perry was holding Amy's small hands between his own larger ones, and they broke apart, neither one able to look again at the other.

"I am sure," Amy managed to say, a little breathlessly, turning away, as if he could see her face drain of colour in the darkness, "that Eve will be glad to see you, for she believed that you were to stay in Naples, I believe, for some time to come."

"Some business with my publishers brought me home earlier than I had expected," he said heavily. "And as soon as I had concluded that in London, I immediately came into Oxford. I lie at the Boar's Head tonight, and I thought, since I could not sleep, that I would take a walk, and see where she lived—your sister, that is!"

"But we are quite five miles from Oxford!"

His smile was beautiful; it seemed to illuminate his face. "But it was such a beautiful night, so full of moonlight, that I immediately began to compose a poem about it, and so I walked and I thought, and before I knew it, I was here. The miles just seemed to slip away."

"Oh, I know just what you mean," Amy replied. "There have been many times when I have been about something, and suddenly struck by a thought, and found myself quite somewhere else for hours after. How much more so it must be when one is a poet."

"'Passing from this dreary vale/Into the regions of my soul,/A landscape undimmed by time—'" Thomas Perry began.

"'Until at last, I am brought home again, whole,/ Undiminished by dreams.'" Amy finished. Her eyes opened wide. "You are the author of that poem? Why, it is one of my favourites!"

"If it is one of *your* favourites, then I must be forever glad to know that I am its humble author," Thomas Perry said modestly.

"Yours are the poems of *The Lonely Wayfarer?*" Amy asked, breathless, and not at all shy in her admiration.

Thomas Perry nodded his head. "My first volume. My second volume is what brought me back from Naples, you see. It is to be called *The Spires of Cambridge,* bound in leather at two and six, from John Murray."

"Oh," Amy said, out of breath. "What an honour it is to meet you. I never thought that *you* would be *that* Thomas Perry. Eve is not at all that poetical, you see."

He shook his dark and handsome head. "No, she is not, is she?" he agreed. "I hope that she will become so, in time."

"But you must tell me how you left Papa. Was he well? When does he expect to come home?"

"Your father is very well indeed, and sends his regards to all. It seems that his excavations have uncovered a new and even more ancient layer, and he may be delayed for some weeks with it. Seems to feel that to judge by the pottery shards and the fragments he'd unearthed, there was far more of a Phoenician influence in Pompeii than he had originally believed, but at a much earlier time than Sir William Hamilton had speculated. The two of them are utterly enthralled with the project, you know, and spent hours and hours at the site."

"How very nice for Papa and Sir William! But you must know that we have crates and crates that he had shipped back already, all of them sitting in the ballroom, waiting to be unpacked."

Thomas Perry gave her his brilliant smile. "That was my second reason for journeying into the country, you know. Sir August was most definite in desiring me to assist you in unpacking and cataloguing his new additions to his collection. He said that you had been his good right hand in such matters."

Amy smiled. "His good right hand! That brings Papa back to me as nothing else could. Although where he proposes to display all of these objects, I do not know! The house is already full to bursting with his treasures, and now we have these crates stacked up in the Gold Salon until it looks like a warehouse!" Smiling, she shook her head. "Sometimes, he reminds me of a small boy with his collection of birds' nests and odd-shaped stones."

"Well, what are statuary fragments but odd-shaped stones?" Thomas Perry asked thoughtfully. "Truly, collectors are a strange lot indeed. Which is not to say of course that your father—"

"Oh, please! Papa is most definitely *a character!* You need not apologise for noting what all the world knows! When my mother died, I think it became his greatest solace, this collecting of objects, for it seems to me that he is always lost in the mists of antiquity."

"And perhaps happier there for the change. Oh, Miss Amy, I went out to Naples in search of inspiration for my work, and indeed, I did find it in the ancient world. The grandest civilizations, you know; when one sits in the hot sun and looks at the ruins of some ancient temple upon a hill, it is almost as if one were there with them."

"You must have had some wonderful inspiration," Amy ventured.

"Oh, yes! I wrote ten or twenty of my most interesting poems during my sojourn there. One that I wrote about an eruption of Vesuvius I particularly liked. Of course, I should like to hone them a bit before presenting them, but I think that it was a wonderful experience, and that I shall never regret the time I spent abroad. But oh, it is wonderful to be back in England again. And in Oxford! I live in Cambridge, you know, so that I have never seen Oxford before, all grey stone and very different from Cambridge, which is more a city of pastels and light. Most interesting!"

"I have never seen Cambridge, but I have always heard that it is a most beautiful city. I was in Bath recently, you see, and I thought that to be quite modern!"

"Bath? Oh, yes. An interesting place, Bath. It was once, I believe, a Roman resort. Quite fashionable, I believe. Beau Nash and all of that." He thought for a moment. "I have an aunt who lives in Bath, now that I recall, and I have been there! Yes! Forgive me. Sometimes, when the force of the muse is upon me, I become quite distracted."

Disarmed by his smile, Amy nodded. "Oh, yes, I quite understand. Well, of course, one's creativity should take precedence over all other events, do you not think so?"

"I suppose. But it does make one rather distracted at times—or so Eve tells me, when I am late or have been diverted."

"Oh, but after years of being with Papa, one would

think that she was used to that. I know I am," Amy replied simply. "'Take hold the fleeting hours, and catch the muse as you may,'" she quoted.

She was rewarded with his look. "My poem 'Gesta'! How you flatter me, Miss Amy!"

"No, it is I who am flattered—to find myself in the company of one of my favourite poets!" Amy replied.

"Then—I don't suppose—no, it is asking too much," Mr. Perry said, shaking his head. "But, Miss Amy, do you think you could bear to listen to the few lines I have written down tonight on the moonlight? I mean to make a sonnet from it, but it's still very rough and not in pentameter quite yet—"

"Nothing would be more exciting!" Amy exclaimed. "Yes, please! I should love to hear your work!"

From his pocket, he withdrew a battered leather notebook, and flipping through its pages, found the lines he wanted. He cleared his throat, then licked the end of his pencil. "'Lines,'" he read, "'By moonlight.'"

For the next three quarters of an hour, Mr. Perry read and reread, and Miss Dartwood listened and suggested.

They sat so close upon the bench that their shoulders touched, and unconsciously, Mr. Perry's free arm rested against the back of the seat, just brushing Amy's shoulders. And yet, their closeness seemed entirely natural and without any suggestion of impropriety. Without either of them recognising it, they had begun to act as if they had been friends forever and ever; it seemed entirely natural to them that they should be thus engaged upon the composition of a poem by moonlight.

It was not until the bell at Seale Abbey tolled matins and lauds that the spell was broken.

Upon the last stroke, Thomas finished, "'Silver Diana, riding across the starry skies.'"

"Wonderful," Miss Dartwood almost whispered admiringly.

"Do you really think so?" Thomas asked. "Then I must say that it was the inspiration of my muse that brought it all about. Would you permit me to dedicate the poem to you, Miss Amy?"

She flushed prettily, but did not deny him his request. "I would be honoured," she said.

Mr. Perry sighed with satisfaction. "On the contrary, it is *I* who am honoured!" From a pocket of his embroidered waistcoat, he withdrew his pocketwatch and frowned. "It is past midnight! I had no idea of the time! Best I should be getting back to the Boar's Head."

"I am sure that you could take one of my sister's hacks—I should hate to wake up the coachman at this hour, but you could just saddle one horse and ride it back tomorrow, if you wish."

"No, no, I shall walk," he said, getting to his feet and offering her his hand to assist her to rise also, holding it just a second longer than necessary.

"This night is drenched in madness, moon madness," Amy whispered. "Tomorrow, when we meet again, we shall be proper and civil people."

"Yes, of course. Daylight has a way of making everything real. Too real for me, sometimes. But it don't signify, as long as I shall see you tomorrow."

"And Eve, of course," Amy said quickly.

"Oh, yes, and Eve, too." Mr. Perry said in the tones of one who has half-forgotten an important fact. "Yes, Eve. Well, Miss Amy—until tomorrow?"

"Until tomorrow," Amy replied.

She watched as he vaulted the wall with an easy grace and disappeared, a faint smile playing about her lips.

Only then did it occur to her that in his presence, she had felt none of the awkward tongue-tied unease she nearly always felt in the presence of gentlemen. And, save for those few odd, and somehow not unpleasant moments when he had kissed her, their whole encounter had been that of two people who had known each other for years—perhaps a lifetime. This was an entirely new sensation to her, and she turned it over in her mind for several moments before she at last made her way into the house.

A bit of moon madness and no more, she thought. Or was it?

Chapter
Eight

SHOES, BOOTS, HATS, BONNETS, shawls, scarves, dresses, and coats were strewn about Eve's room as if a storm had whipped through her bedchamber and left her clothes in its wake.

Eve herself stood before the pier glass in her chemise, holding up first one gown and then another. "*Why* was I born with red hair?" she wailed. "Nothing looks right on me!"

She cast aside a rolled print muslin and picked up an ivory Bombay silk. "Drat the luck!" she cried, just as Amy walked in.

"I was going to say good morning, but it doesn't look as if you're having a very good morning at all," Amy said mildly, picking up a piece of toast from Eve's breakfast tray and spreading jam on it with liberality.

"I can't find anything to wear! Everything looks so dowdy on me, or so silly or something that I can't bear it! And Barras will be here at ten!"

Amy took a bite of her toast. While her sister agitated, she felt a strange sense of peace this morning, as if she had awakened from a wonderful dream. "Such a fuss for Barras, when last night all you could say was odious, odious, odious?" she teased.

"Well, just because he is odious doesn't mean that I must look a dowd and a quiz, does it?" Eve snapped, pushing her hands through her hair. "Oh, I would wear the green-and-white print, but it looks so—so something."

"Nonsense, you will look quite pretty in that," Amy replied, "and I will lend you my white silk Russian caplet with the white roses, and my green-and-white embroidered shawl, and you will look quite nice, I promise you. Anyway, Lord Barras don't signify, because I have the most wonderful surprise for you!"

"The last thing I need right now is a surprise. Where are my yellow slippers? Oh, there they are, under the bed. Jane is going to kill me, I know she is."

"Thomas is here!" Amy could hold her news no longer, so certain was she that it would send her sister into transports of delight.

She was puzzled when Eve looked merely blank for a moment. "Oh, Thomas," she said vaguely, and then, as the light dawned upon her, *"Thomas?"*

"Thomas," Amy agreed, expecting a happy reaction.

"Of all the bad timing!" Eve said, sighing. "It really is too much to ask. Well, I suppose that I shall have to fit him in somehow."

"Aren't you even interested in why he's back and what he's doing?" Amy asked after a moment.

Eve bit her lower lip. "Oh, yes, yes, of course I am! Why would I not be? It is only that it complicates matters, you see. Not that Thomas is complicated, not at all, but with Barras and everything that is going on, I wonder how I shall find the time to see him. Oh, the horror of poets, Amy, you are very lucky that you don't know any."

"But I know Thomas," Amy pointed out, and as Eve dressed and fussed over her appearance with an unwonted vanity, Amy quickly sketched in the events of the previous night. Somewhat to her surprise, Eve seemed less than enthralled with news of her beau. Somewhat to Amy's puzzlement, she seemed to accept his sudden return with no surprise, and less interest than one might have expected from a separated lover. Instead, she tried on several dresses, studying herself this way and that in the mirror, fussed a great deal with her hair, and despaired of her toilette with a nervousness that was so totally unlike her usual self that Amy finally paused to ask her sister if she was feeling quite well.

"Well? Well?" Eve asked. "Of course I feel well! Never felt better in my life! Where are my York tan gloves? I know that Jane put them in the drawer, but I can't find them—oh, here they are, in my hand, where they have been all the time! Should I use just a little powder, do you think, or should I try a little rouge? Don't tell Tabby, she'd die if she knew I had a paint pot, but everyone in Naples does it, and no one can tell. Oh, I hate having freckles! It is so awful!"

Finally, Amy was forced to lay aside her narrative and help her sister to dress, all the while calming her down.

"One would think you had an engagement with the Prince Regent, and not odious Lord Barras," Amy teased mildly as she tied a green sash about the waist of her sister's white cambric dress, and fitted her slender shoulders into a lilac spencer with open froggings of green and white.

"Odious man!" Eve agreed absently, pinching her cheeks until the colour appeared in them.

"What shall I do with Mr. Perry, should he happen to call while you are out?"

"If he wants to uncrate all those boxes I brought back from Italy, then I suggest you put him to it," Eve said, fitting a fetching little white chip-straw toque trimmed with silk ivy and white ribands over her curls.

"Aren't you in the least worried about what he is going to say when he discovers that you are playing me to drive away Lord Barras?" Amy asked.

Their eyes met in the mirror, but neither could fathom the expression of the other. Or perhaps, neither one really wanted to. Although they loved each other as much as always, some invisible line had been drawn between them, and neither could truly see the other's thoughts, thoughts that had once been as easily read as a book.

"You could be me," Eve suggested a little forlornly.

"Absolutely not! He can tell the difference between us."

"Didn't sound as if he could last night! Kissed you, did he?" Eve dipped her little finger into a cloisonné pot and smeared something red on her lips, making a little moue.

"Eve! You really are painting!" Amy exclaimed, much shocked.

"Don't, please, tell Tabby," Eve said. "Anyway, as I said, everyone in Naples does it, and no one thinks anything of it, even the Queen and Lady Hamilton. Well, not that Lady Hamilton counts, but after all, she *is* a famous beauty, whatever else she is."

"Let me try," Amy said, and edged into the pier glass to redden her own lips. "Interesting," she said, after she had studied herself for a moment.

"Yes, it is, and Lady Hamilton says if you are subtle, then no one will ever know that it's paint."

"Fancy that," Amy said, turning her head this way and that to judge the effect. "And from abroad, too."

"Oh, yes, abroad is full of the most amazing things. The Queen told me that you can darken your eyelashes by using Oil of Macassar, but—"

At that moment, there was a tap on the door, and Miss Fisher, in a sober round dress of dove grey, entered the room. She looked about with disapproval at the whirl-wind of disarray, but said nothing about it, much to Eve's relief. Eve was occupied with concealing her tiny con-traband box of lip rouge in a drawer in her dressing table.

"Mr.Perry is downstairs, your fiancé from Naples," she announced. "Tallant put him in the morning room. I had no idea that he was the author of *A Sonnet Upon The Morning Light*. What a very nice young man he is, to be sure! Well-spoken and all that could be called civil!"

"He's charmed Tabby, too," Amy teased, but Eve merely frowned slightly.

"Well, I suppose I must see him, especially since Lord Barras will be here at almost any moment, and it would not do for him to tib our dibs, would it?"

Tabby *tsked* at Eve's use of such language, but made no other comment, which was more than could be said for Jane when she entered the room, a freshly pressed morning gown over one arm.

The three ladies were driven downstairs as much by

the need to receive their guest as by Jane's sharp tongue as she picked up gowns from the floor and found Eve's corals under the washstand.

As they entered the morning room, Mr. Perry rose from his seat. His radiant smile turned to a look of puzzlement as he looked from one twin to the other, and Amy realized that, at first glance, he was unable to distinguish her from her sister.

In the fleeting seconds that followed, she was also able to collect that he was as handsome as she had recalled him in the moonlight. Indeed, perhaps even more so. His dark hair was brushed into the style known as the Brutus, and he was immaculately attired in an elegantly cut coat of bath superfine with a silk waistcoat of tawny and tan stripes. One could have, if one cared to do so, seen his reflection in his gleaming topboots, and his cravat was carefully and perfectly tied in the style known as the *trône d'amour*.

"Ah," he said, simply and eloquently, and immediately moved toward Amy. "My dearest Eve! How lovely you look! And Miss Amy," he said, turning toward Eve to deliver her a slight bow, and a most charming smile.

Before she could stop him, he had once again kissed her. The dreadful thing, to Amy's mind, was that she enjoyed this kiss, public and proper, as much as she had enjoyed his more passionate embrace in the moonlit garden the previous night. A bright flush crept into her cheeks, and she looked down at the toes of her shoes, thrown into utter confusion.

"My lord Barras," Tallant chose to announce at that moment, stepping aside to allow that gentleman to saunter casually into the room.

Amy frantically tried to catch her sister's eye, but it

was of no avail, for Barras was already raising his quizzing glass to his eye to survey the twins.

"As alike as two peas in a pod, they said, and they were correct!" Without a moment's hesitation, he walked up to Eve. "I trust I find you well, Miss Amy?" he asked.

It would have been an easy mistake to make; Eve was dressed for a drive, and Amy wore an ivory morning dress of India muslin, which would indicate she planned no outdoor activities for that morning. Still, it took a little effort for both twins to suppress their sighs of relief. For her part, Miss Fisher made a strangled little sound in the back of her throat that sounded something like the squawk of a parrot, but might have been laughter, for she enjoyed a lively sense of the ridiculous. She concealed it, however, behind a lacey kerchief and a most repressively spinsterish look, and did so very admirably. So much so that Lord Barras dropped his quizzing glass on its ribbon and actually looked just a trifle guilty for having employed this device, offensive as it was to have a greatly magnified eye looking one up and down.

"Good morning, my lord," Eve said smoothly, and no one, not even her own sister, could have detected the least discomfort in the easy manner in which she marched through the situation. "May I present my sister, Miss Eve Dartwood, and her friend, Mr. Perry? And of course, our former governess and present friend and companion, Miss Fisher?"

Lord Barras's coat may have been somewhat in need of pressing and his topboots may have been the despair of his valet, but his manners were very good as he bowed first to the startled Amy, and then to Tabby, followed by a manly nod in the direction of Mr. Perry.

He gave them all his crooked smile. "Forgive me, if

you please," he said in a tone that implied he did not care if they forgave him or not, but was delivered with great charm, "but I have never seen two human beings so alike in almost every aspect! Your servant, Miss Dartwood, Miss Fisher! How d'you do, Mr. Perry! Remarkable! Simply remarkable resemblance, is it not?"

"Yes, but I can tell them apart," Mr. Perry answered, placing a hand upon Amy's. "This is Eve, and that lady is Miss Amy."

Behind her handkerchief, it seemed that Miss Fisher was about to have the vapours, but she composed herself very swiftly into the role of proper chaperone.

"Yes, quite so!" Lord Barras said with a dim flicker of amusement in his dark eyes. "Tell me, sir, you are not Thomas Perry, the poet?"

"I have that honour, Lord Barras. And you, sir, are the famous historian and collector, if my memory serves me well!"

Barras nodded with a grin. "It seems that our reputations have preceded us both! I am not much of a man for poetry, but I must say that when I saw you give a reading in Cambridge last year, I was most affected! Most affected indeed!"

"Thank you, my lord." It was Mr. Perry's turn to smile, and he bowed slightly, giving Amy a droll look as he did so. "How fortunate we are to see you here! Have you come to inspect Sir August's collection of antiquities that he sent back from his Neapolitan excavations? We are about to begin to unpack and catalogue them into his collection."

Barras raised an eyebrow, interested. "No, but, by Jove, I wouldn't mind having a look! I'm certain Sir August has some rare finds!"

"I believe so. We were fortunate enough to excavate

a Pompeiian villa from the ashes, and to find almost everything in the most wonderful condition, were we not, Eve?"

Eve opened her mouth to reply, and Amy, with a slight breathlessness, was quick to respond. "Oh, yes, some very fine things! Urns and—and—"

"I believe you said candelabrums. A fine pair of cast bronze candelabrums!" Eve put in. "I recall you telling me that most distinctly."

"Oh, yes, I did, didn't I?" Amy said a little dizzily.

Miss Fisher was of no use whatsoever; she merely held her handkerchief in front of her face and shook her head from side to side.

"But of course, we can all discuss this later!" Eve said quickly. "Perhaps much later! I am sure that my sister has a great many things she wishes to *explain* to her intended and you have promised me a morning drive, Lord Barras, so perhaps we should not keep the horses waiting!" She seized his arm almost desperately, trying to drag him out of the room, but his attention caught by his favourite subject, Lord Barras was not so easily moved.

"I myself was out in Naples in oh one. A wonderful place, do you not think, Mr. Perry, Miss Dartwood? Of course, you must have seen Vesuvius—we used to pack a hamper and go out to watch it at night. A most thrilling sight, do you not think, Miss Dartwood?"

"Oh, thrilling," Amy agreed in a colourless voice.

"Oh, yes! We were fortunate enough to witness a mild eruption, do you not recall, my dear, and you said to me, what did you say?" Mr. Perry asked fondly of the twin he believed to be Eve.

"I believe she said it was like Wyngate's rockets!" Eve put in, and when everyone stared at her, she added brightly, "It was in one of your letters home to me, ah—Eve."

"Oh yes, yes indeed! We are great correspondents, my sister and I! Why, from her letters, it was almost like being there!" Amy managed to stammer out.

"Well, we can talk about all of this later. I die for a drive! You promised that I might handle the reins today, Lord Barras, and I know you will want to keep your promise," Eve insisted. "Now," she added firmly.

"Yes, of course, just as you say. I never keep a lady waiting, Miss Amy," Barras drawled. "Bad ton, you know." He might have been teasing her. Eve looked at him sharply, but his smile was bland.

"Not even Mrs. Fotherby?" she hissed under her breath in retaliation.

"*Especially* not Mrs. Fotherby," Lord Barras assured her with his most bland smile. "Shall we go? So nice to have met you, Miss Fisher, Miss Dartwood, Mr. Perry."

"What a very nice man," Miss Fisher said when Lord Barras and Eve had left the room. "Really, he did not seem at all imperious to me, Amy—oh!"

As the sound of horses' hooves clipping smartly down the drive echoed in the room, Amy closed the door firmly and turned toward Mr. Perry.

"It's all right, Tabby. Both of us are wretched liars, I fear, although I think it was very wrong of Eve to go off as she did without as much as a word to you, Mr. Perry."

Thomas Perry's smile wavered and he looked genuinely puzzled. "But you are Eve, are you not?"

"No, I am Amy Dartwood," Amy informed him apologetically as Miss Fisher sank into a chair and waved her kerchief before her eyes, obviously done in by so much unaccustomed mendacity. "It is not at all what my father would have approved of, you know," the governess exclaimed, much overwrought. "He was a vicar, you know, and we were not brought up to tell such terrible untruths!"

Amy was quick to comfort her, a little alarmed at this outburst in the usually phlegmatic and prosaic Miss Fisher. "Oh, Tabby, it is all my fault, and I am a very, very wicked girl to allow Eve to continue on with this masquerade!"

Mr. Perry looked from one to the other, his mouth open. The confused workings of his mind could be seen in his expression as he tried to piece things together.

Amy, who was searching among the objects on the cluttered mantel for a vinaigrette she thought she had seen there one or two months ago, was equally flustered. "I am so very sorry, Mr. Perry, but you see, we had no idea that you were coming, and we thought that everything would be resolved by the time Papa was back." Triumphantly, she found the vinaigrette, and uncapped it. "It looks a little dried out," she said dubiously.

Tabby waved it away. "I hope," she said with an attempt at firmness, "that I am not so infirm as to require stimulants."

"Perhaps a little brandy," Thomas Perry suggested, going to the server in the corner of the room and suiting his gestures to his words. He handed a little glass to Miss Fisher and she drank with a weak smile in his direction.

"Thank you! You are very good!" she said. "Which, I am afraid, is more than I can say for this situation! Whatever will Sir August say when he returns? Or Lady Seale!"

"Ah, yes, Lady Seale," Mr. Perry said with a smile as he sat down and began to chafe Tabby's wrists between his hands. "Miss Dartwood, if you would procure a little more brandy, please—yes! I have heard something about

Lady Seale, and I am certain that she is a most formidable female!"

"You don't know the half of that," Amy said as she handed Tabby a second tiny glass of brandy. "And when she finds out, well, it will be dreadful!"

"Then she must not find out!" Thomas declared passionately. "Only, if you please, precisely what is it that she must not find out?"

"Lord Barras!" Tabby moaned. "Mendacity! Oh, dear, abroad must be a dreadful place, for look what it has done to Eve! It has made her more so than ever a headstrong, impetuous girl! Oh, dear, oh, dear! It was very, very wrong of me to consent to this wicked scheme."

"Tabby, please, do not be upset, it is all my fault! If I were not such a wicked, cowardly girl, none of this would have happened!"

"Ladies, please! Before you indulge in any more mutual recriminations, I must know what is going on!" Thomas exclaimed. "Perhaps," he added, "I might even be able to help you!"

Both Tabby and Amy turned toward him as if he were their knight in shining armour. The presence of male authority clearly left them impressed and hopeful.

"You see, I went to Bath, and my Aunt Seale, you see, and I had the influenza, and she thought that it would do me some good to drink the waters, only we happened to meet Lord Barras, and he took it into his head that since I was Sir August's daughter, a match between us would be a very good thing, except he terrifies me, you see, so arrogant and so toplofty." Amy paused for breath.

Amazingly enough, Mr. Perry seemed perfectly able to follow this narrative, and nodded encouragingly. "Please, continue!" he begged her.

"Well, you see, somehow or another, Lord Barras thought that I agreed to marry him, although what I said was *Awk!* or *Awp!* perhaps, but not yes! *Never* yes!" Amy cried in increasing agitation. "But you see, Aunt Seale despaired of my sister and I *ever* getting married and she pressed so very hard, and although she meant well, I was still terrified, so then when she invited him to come and stay at Seale Abbey, I was in a panic, you see, because I did not know what to do! And then Eve came home, and you see, she is stronger-willed than I am, and she decided that she would be me, only she would be me in such a dreadful way that Lord Barras would cry off instantly! So, he took her for a drive in his phaeton yesterday, thinking that *she* was *me,* and when she came in yesterday afternoon all she could do was rave, the way Eve does, you know."

"Oh, yes, I know! She has a rare temper!" Mr. Perry agreed, shaking his head. "It is, if you will forgive me for saying so, one of her less attractive traits! But I interrupt! Pray continue!"

"She ranted and had something of a tantrum, really, threw her hat across the room and called him an out-and-outer, which I am not precisely certain what it means, but I imagine it is not at all kind, and she said that she had tried everything to give him such a disgust of her, well, of me, really, you see, that he would cry off immediately! But he didn't seem in the least to feel that it signified, and well, when you came in today, she was dressing to go out to do battle with him again! She truly believes that if she can give him enough of a horror of her, well, of me, really, that he will be driven away from us forever."

Amy turned enormous green eyes upon Mr. Perry and appeared very near the verge of tears. Unlike many females, she was extremely beautiful when she cried, and Mr. Perry was certainly not impervious to her beauty.

"I think I begin to see! Most inconvenient of me to appear, was it not?" he asked, shaking his head. He sighed. "I suppose she will take my head for washing for coming without announcing myself, but dash it, how was I to know what scheme she had embroiled herself in this time?"

"This time?" Miss Fisher asked suspiciously.

"Well, Eve has a way of getting into tangles, you know. She means well, but sometimes she can be a very managing sort of female. The time in Naples when she— but never mind that!" He formed a rueful smile and spread his fingers, long and elegant, in an expressive gesture. "No, I am not surprised at her conduct, precisely, but disappointed, yes! I had hoped that back in England, she would—well, it doesn't bear speaking of, and I hope you will forgive me."

"Oh, but I know precisely what you are saying. It would be very hard not to, you know, for she is my twin, and it was my wretched cowardice that led to this present tangle, so I must be entirely to blame. Eve is only being a loyal sister to me," Amy said, eyes downcast.

"No, no, you must not say you are a coward!" Mr. Perry protested. "A gently reared lady, sensible and genteel, and unaccustomed to the forthright manners of such a man as Lord Barras could have acted in no other way. I am sure his lordship is an honourable man, but he is, you know, very fashionable, and his manners are those of a cynical society. You must not judge yourself too harshly, Miss Amy!" he exclaimed with passion in his voice, and expressed such finely developed feelings that Amy could not help but look at him gratefully. In a most comforting manner, he placed one hand over her own and gazed sincerely into her eyes. "To be sure, if I had been in your position, I should have felt precisely the same!"

"W-would you?" Amy asked, held enraptured by the blue depths of his gaze.

"Naturally! I, myself, have always been a great admirer of sensibility in a female."

"Oh," Amy said.

A delicate and not unbecoming flush crept into her cheeks and she smiled an uncertain little smile, like the sun coming out from behind the clouds.

"Now," Mr. Perry said gently, "that is better. Since I know that nothing I could say or do will stop Eve once she has made up her mind, only tell me what we may do in the meantime to mitigate her worst excesses. Someone ought to tell Lord Barras the truth, do you think? Should you need a knight for such a mission, I believe that I could fulfill it for you."

"Oh, no!" Amy protested. "That would never do! If he did not put the story out everywhere, Aunt Seale would be certain to discover it, and then where would we all be? The scandal of it all would ruin us both!"

Amy looked so distressed that Thomas felt obliged to hold her hand within his own. "Now, I am certain it will not come to anything so dreadful as all of that! Whatever tangle Eve has gotten herself into, she has always managed to extricate herself from again, but I do wish she would not do so!" He shook his head. "I only wish she would listen to me," he added a little glumly.

Amy was about to say that her sister listened to no one, then decided that was uncharitable and bit her lip.

Mr. Perry's temper was sanguine, however, and his intellect, when not preoccupied with his poetry, prosaic. He merely shook his head. "Well, I am sure that one way or another, Eve will manage," he said after a moment's reflection. "She always has before, you know. Although," he added, "Lord Barras seems to be perfectly capable of handling her himself. My question now is what I may do to be of service to you, Miss Amy. I cannot bear to see you so distraught."

"I feel so much better now that you are here," Amy said, sighing. "Somehow, I do not feel as if disaster loomed over our heads!"

"You flatter me, Miss Amy," Mr. Perry said. "Well, it would seem to me that there is very little we can do while Eve is out jaunting around the countryside with Lord Barras, so perhaps we ought to occupy ourselves with Sir August's mission. There are a great many things that need to be uncrated and I am most anxious to assure myself that a certain krater arrived unbroken."

"Oh, yes! So much better to turn one's hand to something one can do than something one is powerless over. Oh, Mr. Perry, you *are* clever," Amy said with a sigh, allowing him to help her to her feet.

"Not clever at all! I am, I fear, the most unworldly of fellows, or so my students tell me at Cambridge. I have always made a policy of leaving cleverness to people who enjoy that sort of thing!"

"Dear Tabby, will you be all right?" Amy inquired solicitously of her governess.

Miss Fisher, who had been watching this interchange silently, adjusted her cap strings and nodded courageously. "Of course," she said. "I shall inform Tallant that we are to be five for lunch, and that you will want the estate carpenter with his tools in the drawing room."

After they had disappeared down the hallway, giggling like a pair of children, Miss Fisher did something unheard of for her; she rose and poured herself another thimbleful of brandy.

Returning to her seat, she looked at it for several moments. All serenity had left her expression, just as she felt that all control had slipped from her hands in the matter of her formal pupils.

One could not, of course, help but *dislike* a situation in which one twin impersonated the other, and one had always deplored such, well, pranks in the past. And, one had really hoped that the twins had long outgrown such antics.

In a way, she had hoped that their separation would reinforce the twins' independence from each other, for she had always believed that their closeness precluded any great hope of achieving a desirable state of marriage for either one, and as Lady Seale had pointed out, the alternative—a spinsterly existence on what Sir August would leave them—would have been at best, shabby-genteel poverty. What Miss Fisher had not hoped for was that each one's worst characteristics would be reinforced by the separation; that Amy would become more shy and retiring and Eve entirely too bold. But that was what she saw happening, and she could not help but wonder what the outcome of all this would be. Clearly, Lord Barras was far too forceful a personality for Amy, while Mr. Perry was plainly no match for Eve. But, she thought, suppose, just suppose . . .

It was too much to hope for, whatever her thought had been. She tossed down her brandy and shook her head.

"Those girls will drive me mad yet," she said, sighing. "Not yet noon and I am drinking hard spirits already!"

Chapter
Nine

"THE CAT SEEMS TO have your tongue this morning," Lord Barras remarked after they had driven several miles in silence.

Eve, who had been waiting for her heart to stop beating like thunder in her breast, managed a weak smile. "Oh, I suppose I am thoughtful today. I am a creature of quicksilver moods, you know, and prone to being a watering pot as much as a chatterbox." Even as she spoke, she was aware of a strong feeling of self-disgust, for she had begun to dislike having to represent herself to this man as a thoroughly unpleasant person. How could Thomas have simply appeared like that, she raged, at the very worst possible moment? It was so like him, and his poetical nature to simply show up without as much as a word of warning! In Naples, it had seemed very romantic. But somehow, here in England, it was merely annoying. She could only hope that Amy and Tabby had managed to explain everything to his satisfaction, and she dreaded returning, for she would have to give him a long and critical explanation of her conduct that he would doubtless moralise upon in a rather dreary way. It was, she reflected, a great deal too bad that his scruples were so fine. It occurred to her that had the situation been reversed, Lord Barras would have fallen in happily with the scheme. Odious man, she reminded herself, but felt it a distinctly half-hearted thought. Far from the ogre she had expected him to be, he was bright and witty, intelligent and competent. Amy was a bit of a ninny, she admitted to herself, to think Barras such a monster for knowing his own mind and speaking it. She suddenly felt thoroughly confused.

"Perhaps you might like to take the reins?" Lord Barras offered. "That might take you out of your brown study."

Such an offer was too much for Eve to resist and she replied with enthusiasm, "Oh, yes, please!" All of her thoughts were forgotten as she wrapped the reins about her fingers and set the handsome team into the trot, she smiled brilliantly.

Freed of his concentration, Lord Barras leaned back against the perch and rested on his elbows, watching as she guided the horses. He made no comment upon her skills, but smiled a lazy smile.

"You know," he remarked conversationally, "One often hears about twins being identical, but one rarely, if ever, actually sees it."

"Oh, yes," Eve agreed easily, "Many people find it hard to tell my sister and I apart."

"I imagine that as children, you were forever playing

tricks upon the unsuspecting. It must have been great fun," he added.

Eve smiled. "We used to do such things. Our nanny could not tell us apart, you know, so she dressed us differently—I wore blue and my sister wore pink. I am afraid that we used to be quite inventive in the ways in which we chose to plague people when we learned that no one could tell us apart."

"I am an only child, you know. No brothers and sisters at all. I wonder what it would be like to have an exact double."

"For myself, I have often wondered what it would be like to be a singleton."

"I assume you and your sister are close?"

"Until—until she went to Naples, we were never separated. And then we were part for eighteen months. It is not such a bad thing, you know, as I first thought it would be. Both of us managed to attain our own identity in some way, I think. I know I did, and I *sense* that she did, although it is not something we have discussed."

Lord Barras said nothing more for a while, and when Eve happened to glance over at him, he seemed to be lost in some thought that amused him deeply, for his lips were curved upward in a smile.

She had all that she could do to handle the team, fresh and high-spirited, and she gave over her complete attention to the horses. When he spoke again, asking her opinion of Belzoni's excavations in the tombs of the Egyptian pharaohs, she was able to reply with some light comment, not having kept abreast of the explorer's adventures and discoveries.

Lord Barras, however, had followed them all with great interest, and for the next quarter hour was able to tell her as much about them as he knew.

He spoke with such interest that Eve was impelled to ask him, "Have you ever thought of mounting an expedition yourself?"

Barras smiled his crooked, oddly charming smile. "Frequently!" he exclaimed. "In fact, when I was with Mountforte in ninety-six, out in the jungles of Central America, I made a vow that I should return. There is said, mind you, to be a lost city somewhere deep in the jungles of the Yucatan Peninsula that no European has ever seen—and few Indians. It could have been one of the greatest cities of the ancient Mayan culture, and, if it exists, lies buried under tons and tons of jungle and earth, but think of what discoveries may be lying there! We know so little about the ancient Mayans, and so much could be discovered. They had pyramids, you know, like the Egyptians, and an entire pantheon of deities that we believe may be similar to those of Egypt—" he broke off, shaking his head. "But I am boring you! I forget that you are not at all interested in antiquities, but prefer everything to be modern."

His tone was teasing, but Eve was sensitive to her own heedlessness. She was interested, and very much so, in what he had to say about Mountforte's expedition, and realised that she had buried herself with her own tongue.

"Odious man," she said, but her tone was half-hearted, and almost teasing. Unhappily, she realised that she was warming to him in spite of herself, and attempted to steel her reserves back into the character she had invented. Poor, dear, silly Amy! To be cowed by a man such as this. Arrogant he might be, and too frank with his thoughts, but an ogre—well, he seemed to her to be less than that.

Confused, she threw her concentration into the team and was surprised when he pulled the reins from her hands abruptly. "Ho!" he cried, bringing them to a dead stop.

"I was handling them perfectly well!" she cried, offended by his high-handedness.

But he seemed not to hear her as he jumped down easily from the high perch and slid himself with agility under the traces to inspect the hooves of his right leader.

"Hold 'em steady!" he commanded, and she picked up the reins again automatically.

"What's wrong?" she cried.

"He's thrown a shoe. Look back in the road and you can see it lying there. Damn!"

Eve craned her neck to look, and indeed, did see a single horseshoe lying forlornly in the road. The team, high-strung and nervous, grew restive, and it was all she could do to hold them still while Barras bent over the horse, speaking softly to it as he inspected its hoof.

"Is there a village about with a blacksmith?" he asked her. "Somewhere within walking distance?"

Eve nodded. "Hathaway is about a mile distant over the hill. There's a smith there."

Barras nodded. "Good. We'll walk them there, if you think you can manage it. I know you hate to walk."

"Hand me down," Eve commanded. "I am not made of cotton wool, you know."

Barras gave her a funny look, but contented himself with saying, "No, I did not think you were."

He watched as she clambered down unassisted from the high perch, and if he appreciated the sight of a finely turned ankle in the process, he merely grinned and said nothing as Eve took one bridle and he took the other and they began to walk the team down the road toward Hathaway.

*　*　*

Long afternoon shadows fell through the high, curtained windows of the drawing room, its subtle, orderly furnishings covered with a layer of highly disorganised clutter. Wads of sawdust strips lay everywhere, and the dissembled skeletons of crates and cartons were scattered about the Axminster rugs like soldiers on an ancient battlefield.

In the middle of all this clutter, illuminated by the late afternoon sunlight that touched them with golden highlights, sat Thomas and Amy, gazing with rapture upon a single object they had placed on a table.

It was a krater urn perhaps a foot tall, and in almost perfect condition in spite of its long burial in the ashes of Pompeii. The paint was as brilliant as it had been the day that city was destroyed, and the small figures that merrily pursued each other around its sides were, to its two admirers, as alive as themselves.

"I think perhaps it may have been a Grecian import," Mr. Perry was saying. His shirt was no longer white, but coated with yellow dust, and his points were sadly wilted, but he was oblivious to anything but its beauty as he gazed upon the ancient object.

Amy, her muslin dress covered with a smock, a streak of black dirt smudging her pale complexion, sat with a notebook in her lap. It was filled with notes taken in her neat, round hand, and she still held the pencil in her fingers as she gazed at the urn.

It was illuminated by a shaft of light, and seemed to glow faintly.

"Only think," she whispered reverently, "it is two thousand years old, and perhaps more."

"Or perhaps a little less, but what difference?" Mr. Perry mused. "If it had a voice, what could it tell us?"

They looked up at each other in sudden acknowledgement of a mutual thought.

"What a wonderful poem that would make," Amy said softly.

"Yes," Mr. Perry said. "But what a far more beautiful poem I could write about you, gazing enraptured upon this vase at this very moment. Miss Amy, you are a beautiful woman."

Amy smiled, pleased. "Do you think so?" she asked. "Many people do not like ginger hair."

"Then many people are great fools," Thomas said softly. "In this light, your hair is like a sunset, you know."

Automatically, Amy reached up to touch her curls. Her green eyes met Mr. Perry's ice-blue ones, and suddenly, as if both struck by the same thought, they looked away.

"One krater urn," Mr. Perry said in a much more businesslike voice, "Twelve and three-quarter inches high, eighteen and seven-eighths inches wide, hand-thrown on a wheel, painted in shades of black and terra-cotta red. Circled by figures in some sort of dance, most of them female and bearing garlands of flowers. Two of them playing flutes, one of them with a lyre." With subtle hands he turned the vase about, and Amy dutifully made notes as he spoke. "It would appear that one of the female figures is a presentation of the goddess Diana, for she wears animal skins and carries a bow and arrow. In her hair, she wears an ornament with the crescent moon. She seems to be receiving the paeans of the musicians, as well as offerings of fruit and flowers from other figures. A most unusual piece."

". . . a most . . . unusual piece . . ." Amy dutifully

scribed. She leaned back in her chair and looked about the room. "I do not know where Papa intends to put all of these things. The house is full to bursting with his collections now." With her pencil, she waved a careless hand about the room, which indeed was already full of statuary of the classical period.

Idly, Thomas picked up a pair of brass plates and turned them over in his hands. He was about to say something else when the door burst open and Eve, flushed and disheveled, rent the sombre sunlit silence.

"I am so sorry we missed lunch!" she exclaimed at once, stirring up whorls of sawdust as she moved across the carpet, "but we had a horse throw a shoe, and the Hathaway smith was out at someone's farm, and we had to wait for him to return, and we ate a cold luncheon at the most charming little inn. They had a baby lamb, you see, and I could not resist feeding it with a pap bowl, and Gervase—Lord Barras bought it for me, so now we have a lamb in the stables, and I must think of a name for it. Of course Crossley—our head groom, Thomas—is *aux anges* at me for bringing a lamb home, but they were going to slaughter it, and I could not bear that, however heartless some people think I am."

Lord Barras, more disheveled than ever, strolled in behind her, his hands thrust into his pants pockets and a sheepish grin on his face.

"I have persuaded her that it will be much happier on Lady Seale's home farm, where it will doubtless grow into a very large and very stupid old ewe and the mother of many sheep to come, but I am afraid Tallant was sorely put out when I suggested it might be given the run of the house. I say, what a fine urn you have there, may I?"

At their entrance, Thomas and Amy had moved

guiltily apart, but neither Eve nor Barras seemed to notice, any more than Thomas and Amy noted the air of companionable intimacy that seemed to exist between the eldest Miss Dartwood and the man she had castigated not twenty-four hours before as *odious,* and had vowed to remove from their lives forever.

As Barras studied the urn, discussing it in low tones with Mr. Perry, Eve drew off her gloves and her cap and tossed them idly on a chair, saying, "Oh, by the way, what do you think of Gervase staying to dinner? I challenged him to a chess match, since he thinks he is the grand expert in the game. Thomas, you will stay to dinner, will you not?"

He threw her a calm, almost bemused look. "I should be delighted," he said, before answering some point Barras had raised about the design of the handles on the urn.

"You did explain it all to him, did you not?" Eve asked Amy in an undertone.

Amy nodded. "He took it better than I expected he would, but really, Eve—"

"Oh, Thomas will be stuffy, but don't worry," Eve replied airily. "Poor Tabby, she was almost beside herself when we were not back for lunch, she was so ready to believe that I had landed us both in a ditch somewhere with a broken neck. You would think that after all of this time, she would know that I am fully capable of driving to an inch."

"Just barely! Perhaps driving to a half-foot!" Barras shot at her, and Eve gave him a wicked grin, not at all offended.

"Odious man," she said in tones that were almost affectionate.

Speechless, Amy could only stare from one of them to the other, and Thomas Perry merely smiled tolerantly.

After Amy had recovered herself, she ventured, a little hesitant, "E-Amy, I thought that since Aunt Seale continues to be away, and Lord Barras has already been given the run of the Abbey, perhaps it would be better if Thomas were to move his things from the Boar's Head up to the Abbey. After all, Papa particularly requested him to assist me in cataloguing his new acquisitions, and it would be so much more convenient."

"Oh, I am certain that would be very nice, Mr. Perry would be most welcome, think you not, Tabby? It would quite be like old times, when Cousin Timothy was at university and used to fill the house with his friends during the long holiday. Barras, what say you? How did this urn, so obviously Greek and so obviously first century, come to be in a Pompeiian household? Spoils of war or a true collector?"

Chapter
Ten

"I REALLY *DO* WISH you would say something!" Eve finally expostulated after a very long silence.

Thomas Perry selected a rose from the nearest bush and snapped it off at the joint of the stem. He inhaled its moist perfume, then placed it carefully into his lapel with a look of satisfaction that would have thrilled Eve in Naples but now served to drive her near distraction. Oblivious, or apparently so, he turned his head slightly over his shirt points to gaze at her impassively, his pale-blue eyes unreadable. "I was thinking that roses deserve a poem of their own. I must tell your gardener so, what was his name? MacDonald?"

"MacDowell, and I do wish you wouldn't just walk

about like a stick and not say anything, when I know you are dying to have at me."

Mr. Perry shook his head slightly. "I think you know what I feel about this masque," he said evenly.

"Well, it couldn't be helped," Eve said stiffly, tilting her head slightly upward toward the faintly grey afternoon sky.

The luncheon party had broken up; Lord Barras claimed pressing business in Oxford, and Amy and Miss Fisher, with more concern than grace, had discovered an urgent need to discover the whereabouts of some chickenfoot jelly receipts mislaid by the housekeeper. Thus left alone, Eve Dartwood and her future fiancé, Thomas Perry, strolled about MacDowell's well-tended domains. It was the best they could do for privacy.

But a casual observer, watching their stroll through the rose garden toward the boxwood topiary, might have mistaken them for strangers, so unloverlike was their behaviour. Perhaps it was the weather, which in a move typical of an English June had turned from a balmy morning into a grey and somewhat overcast afternoon, promising a misty shower of rain before teatime. In Italy, the weather had always been remarkably clement, full of warmth and sunshine, the landscape rich with the foliage of bright, Mediterranean colours that almost hurt the eye. Here, everything was misty and restrained, cast in pastel shades and dainty shapes. In this cold climate, no exotic passion flowers would ever bloom.

Miss Dartwood, a little annoyed that she did not seem to be achieving the reaction she longed for in her beau, frowned and twirled the delicate malacca handle of her parasol, pressed upon her by Miss Fisher in an effort to keep her skin from tanning even further. What Eve wanted was a violent emotion, a lover's explosion in which grief could be aired on both sides, to be followed by a sweet and sensual reconciliation that would leave all mended and forgiven; that, to put it simply, was her nature. What she had was Thomas Perry, whose character was far from volatile and whose essential nature was phlegmatic and contemplative, as befit a successful poet and Cambridgian scholar.

But even Thomas's peaceful nature was strained by the day's events, and he sighed in annoyance. "I was, of course, prepared to love your sister as if she were my own," he said slowly and thoughtfully, "and now that I have met her, I can successfully say that I shall have no trouble entertaining those sentiments toward her. She is in every way a most delightful female, and an excellent person with many fine qualities about her, not the least of which is her modesty, which I find becoming in a woman of breeding. I can well understand your desire to protect her from the unwelcome advances of a gentleman whose courtship she does not desire, although I, myself, upon casual knowledge of Barras, find him an agreeable enough sort, if a bit careless in his dress and high-handed in his manner—"

"He is not high—"

"If you please, Eve! Let me finish!" Mr. Perry said firmly. "What I cannot, however, understand, is your childish impetuosity in allowing yourself to be such a shatterbrain as to enact the scheme of impersonating your sister in order to dissuade Barras from his suit! Doing it a bit too brown, Eve, in short!"

She knew there was truth in what he said, but somehow she had expected him to support her, rather than deliver her a lecture, and she felt a stab of disappointment. Worse than that, she hated more than anything not only to be wrong, but to have this pointed out to her.

"Such levity is all very well in Naples, I think, where things are very much different. Every night was like a masqued ball, there, you recollect, and standards were much more relaxed! But there, of course, things are different than here."

"An astute observation!" Eve murmured sarcastically.

"Eve," Thomas said with a sigh, rubbing the bridge of his nose between thumb and forefinger and shaking his head. "You know precisely what I mean! I had hoped that when you were back in England, you would—"

"Behave myself!"

"That too," he said thoughtfully, frowning as he looked off in the distance. "But mostly, I had hoped that your spirit would be turned into more practical channels! Recall that not only am I a poet, but also a teacher, and that as a don's wife, you would be expected to comport yourself with a certain dignity, as would befit your role."

It was not as if he was presenting her with fresh news; they had discussed his career and her future part in it often enough beneath the warm Italian stars. At the time, it had all seemed terribly romantic; now it seemed merely restrained and confining. And the one thing Eve's spirit would not stand was confinement.

Nonetheless, she looked down at the toes of her striped ivory and celestial blue satin slippers and bit back her protesting words. "You are right," she said. "I am a wicked, wicked girl, and Tabby is right, no good will come out of this at all!"

"Now you are being commonsensical," Mr. Perry said, taking her hand and placing it in the crook of his elbow. "I think the best thing for you to do would be to make a clean breast of it all to Lord Barras and have done, instead of continuing to encourage him, as you have been doing."

"But I haven't been encouraging him at all!" Eve protested. "In fact, I have been the most obnoxious, odious, ghastly creature you could imagine!"

"Dearest Eve! You could *never* be so!" Thomas said fondly. "Not in a thousand years!"

"You don't know," Eve replied darkly, but Mr. Perry did not seem to hear her.

"Now, it seems to me, upon brief knowledge, that Barras isn't the sort of fellow who's likely to press his suit where it's not wanted! The fellow may have his quirks, but he's not a loose fish, you know, not a Barras of Highgrove! Quite a respectable family, after all. His uncle is dean of St. Celthois College, and a noble scholar on medieval theology. I am certain that if you and Amy were to make a clean breast of it all, he would be willing to accept it as a joke, and quite naturally forgive you both!"

"Then you don't know him or my sister, Thomas!" Miss Dartwood exclaimed. "His pride is such that we would never be able to hold our reputations again, and Amy's dread of any unpleasantness is so intense that she would doubtless run away from home before having to face his anger! Don't you see, Thomas? My way *is* best. We'll let him stay on for a day or so longer, and then, when he does propose, I'll let him down gently and he will go away. Thomas, do you really believe that I am enjoying this?" Eve asked, holding the brim of her hat as she turned her face up to his to look at him.

"Yes, as a matter of fact, I think you are," Mr. Perry replied a bit sadly.

"I am not! Not a bit!" Eve insisted. "Dearest Thomas, I know I have been foolish in this scheme, but you do see, don't you, that it was for Amy's sake that I did it all? And that it is for Amy's sake that I must continue to play this *stupid* charade out to its finish?"

"Life, my dear, is not like the plot of some silly opera at the San Carlo. I only wish you could understand that." He looked down at her tenderly, and smiled, shaking his head.

"I know it's not like an opera plot, and sometimes I wish it were! Then everything would have a happy ending and things would go just as one wished!"

"*Don Giovanni*," he reminded her, "did not end happily at all."

"Well, that is because he was a very bad man who went about seducing a great many females who should have known better, and killed a man. Gothick and fustian!" Eve brightened a little. "Besides, did you know that Barras has a mistress, a Mrs. Fotherby? If that doesn't make him like Don Giovanni, then I don't know what does! Perhaps some giant statue will come and drag *him* off to—"

"No, I did not know that Barras had a mistress, and neither should you! That is the sort of thing I mean, Eve! Your mind has the most deplorable tendency not just to wander off in the oddest directions, but to discuss the most improper subjects! Maria Carolina almost fainted dead away when you mentioned—"

"Fustian! It would have taken a great deal more than the mention of that old scandal to shock her! Why, she's as tough as chestnuts, and a daughter of Maria Theresa besides, and if there was not a female more hard-minded than her, then you may call me pigeon pie and eat me up!"

Much like Lady Seale, Miss Fisher and Amy Dartwood, Mr. Perry threw his hands up in the air in a gesture that was half exasperation and half defeat. Like those worthy mentors, he exclaimed, "What am I going to do with you?"

"Anything," Eve replied evenly, "but call me pigeon pie and eat me up. Anyway, it is for Amy's sake, it is not some mischievous scheme I dreamt up to amuse myself, not this time, at any rate. Dearest, dearest Thomas, do say that you'll let me carry on as things stand. It will only be for a little while, I promise, and then he'll be so happy to leave us all that you couldn't believe."

Clearly, Mr. Perry was wavering in the face of charm and the cause of Miss Amy Dartwood. Sensing her advantage, Eve pressed on. She wheedled, she cajoled and she pleaded, painting such an affecting portrait of her sister as a maiden in deep distress that in the end Mr. Perry was forced to surrender.

"Oh, very well," he conceded at last. "But I warn you, Eve Dartwood, you need not expect me to tolerate any more of this foolishness once we are married!"

However, when he returned with her to the house and announced his cooperation, the look of gratitude and hero worship on Amy Dartwood's expressive countenance was payment in rich currency.

"Dear, dear Mr. Perry!" she exclaimed, gazing up at him adoringly, in the way in which he had always wanted Eve to do, but she never really had, "I knew you would be kind and good and noble and brave! Now, we cannot fail with you on our side!"

"At last, I may feel sanguine," Miss Fisher said, sighing with relief. "Mr. Perry, a man's influence is so sorely needed in this household—I need say no more! But I know Sir August would be most grateful if he knew the interest you had taken in our affairs at Dartwood House!"

Since Sir August had never seemed to take a great interest in the affairs of his daughters when he was in residence, this might have been construed as preposterous hyperbole by anyone who did not understand the extent of Miss Fisher's adoration of her employer. But Mr. Perry, whose admiration for the antiquarian scholar was almost as great as Miss Fisher's, merely nodded in agreement.

To be sure, the triple gaze of three admiring females upon him was a new and heady sensation for Thomas Perry. The youngest and least significant—at least in his hearty father's eyes—of a number of sporting sons, he was not used to adoration. In spite of his romantic poetry, his life at Cambridge was so exclusively segregated that he rarely had the chance to be spoiled by admirers of the opposite sex. To be sure, such things were exhilarating, but so trusting were the Dartwood sisters and their mentor that he rose admirably to the event, saying modestly, "I shall do whatever there is in my power to assist you!"

Happily for all concerned, he was not called upon to practise too much mendacity. His days were agreeably passed in the company of Amy Dartwood, perusing ancient objects and pursuing his muse. He found Amy to be a most inspirational companion of the chase.

He could find no fault with her demeanour, and thought her shyness most pleasing, as it created in his bosom a manly desire to shelter and protect her from the torrents and buffets of the real world. He admired her creativity and her placid air of domesticity, applauded her sensitivity and roundly admired her scholarly discipline and intelligence. If he found, from time to time, that he wished Eve possessed more of her sister's rectitude and reflective qualities, at no time was he seized with the *presque vu* that might reasonably have been expected to follow such emotions. Nor, it seemed, did Amy enjoy any sudden revelations.

As day after day passed, each one bringing the cartering firm up the drive with yet a new load of crates and boxes from Naples, all of them demanding to be unpacked, evaluated and sorted out, their routine settled into a sort of quiet harmony that both of them seemed to find no fault with, and indeed a great deal of pleasure. But whether the pleasure came from the time spent in each other's company or the joy of discovering another person of similar outlooks and interests, it would have been hard to say.

Certainly, they were so preoccupied in their own world that they barely seemed to note that the visit of Lord Barras stretched several days, then weeks past what he had originally intended.

Nor did Eve seem particularly anxious to dismiss him. Having found a companion mentally and physically as active as herself, she barely noted the gradual erosion of her sham abrasiveness into the jocular ease of confident friendship.

Here, at last, was a person who could match her every move, who enjoyed the give and take as much as she did, and who could give as good as he got. Rather than deploring her spirit, he encouraged her, often outrageously, to do and say what she thought, and was always just a step ahead of her.

From the time he arrived in the morning shortly after breakfast until he took his departure long after dinner, Gervase Barras was able to accomplish something Eve believed no one, not even her sister, had ever been able to; he never, ever *bored* her. For a woman who had long been kept under the constraints of an almost excessive propriety, the freedom that Barras's presence offered Eve was as heady and intoxicating as had been her first glass of champagne (perhaps more so!).

He took her driving, and trusted her so much with his team that her skills improved to a great extent. Barras only half-regretfully remarked that it seemed a shame that he could not propose her for membership in the Four Horse Club, as she was a better whip than many who enjoyed that privilege, including the Prince of Wales himself.

They rode together after lunch, over the fields and along the hedgerows, each one testing the other's mettle and energy with a grudging admiration. Barras spoke freely to her about his hunting, and the great Irish hunts he had participated in, in such a way as to make her yearn for autumn. Although she rode to hounds, her own hunting had been severely curtailed by Aunt Seale, who considered it unfeminine to hunt too often, as it often left one too exhausted for the ballroom and the drawing room. Unfortunately, Mr. Perry was not a great horseman.

Lord Barras challenged Eve to games of battledore and shuttlecock, at which she beat him quite as often as he defeated her, the pair of them darting madly about the south lawn, racquets in hand, in relentless and serious pursuit of the little white feathered birdie, engaged in a combat so fierce that MacDowell was heard to grumble that they were tearing up his finely manicured grass with their antics.

In the long afternoons, as Amy and Thomas excavated their crates of shards and rusted iron, the long golden glow of the afternoon light echoed with the cries of the victor and the defeated on the lawn.

"It is unfair! You lobbed that shot out of my court!"

"Pottery fragment with handle, kiln-fired terra-cotta with the face of a medusa, six inches by approximately three and a half inches."

"I did no such thing! You merely missed an open shot I practically *delivered* to you as a gift! A blind man could have seen that coming!"

"Ivory figurine, oh, look, Thomas, how beautiful it is! It looks like an Egyptian cat! Now, you know, in that sonnet, after 'arched spires and pediments royal,' you could say something like 'dawn crept through the stone like an Egyptian cat,' and that would fit beautifully with the first couplet."

Lord Barras was pleased to discover that Lady Seale had a fine and very much underused trout stream running through her property, and decided it was a great shame that the poachers should have all the fun. Mr. Perry firmly declared himself no sportsman, and Amy shuddered at the thought of impaling anything on a hook, even a feather fly, but Eve seized quite happily upon the notion of learning how to fish, and, attired in her oldest clothes and sturdiest oilskin boots, stood among the reeds at the edge of the stream allowing Lord Barras to show her how to cast with the delicate, whip-like bamboo poles.

It had been a week of rain, and sunlight filtered softly through the pale and watery sky when Lord Barras gently eased himself up against Eve's back, guiding his arms up beneath her own so that their elbows rested one on top of the other's.

"Now," he said gently, his breath light and warm against her neck, the smell of him—clean shirts and pale cologne—in her nostrils as he placed the rod in her hands, "the trick is all—in the—wrists." As he spoke, his hands covered hers, guiding her cast out across the smoothly running water. As he loosened the pin on the reel, the line unspooled with a singing sound and the dabbled fly sailed out across the surface of the stream, skittering across the surface with the grace of a ballet dancer.

"Now," he went on, "very gently, you pull it back and begin to wind in your line—"

"Like this?" Eve asked, trying to follow his instructions. As she spoke, she instinctively turned toward him, to read his expression.

His face was breathtakingly close to hers, and she suddenly found herself gazing into the dark and bottomless depths of his eyes.

A smile, no more than the flicker of a diabolical grin, curved his lips as he moved his face toward hers, lightly brushing her cheek with his mouth.

Eve stiffened for a second, feeling his muscular chest pressing firmly against her back, his strong arms about her. She attempted to struggle free of his embrace, but there was no escape. Nor, in the next second, did she wish for escape, as he pressed his mouth roughly, hungrily against hers.

She felt her knees weaken and a delicious surrendering *frisson* passed through her body as she responded to his kiss, turning in his arms to face him, allowing herself to be enveloped within the protective power of his arms as she gave herself over to her feelings, reaching up, with her free arm, to touch the back of his neck.

Eve had been kissed before, but nothing, not even Thomas's embraces, had ever made her feel as if she were a liquid tide of molten fire, hungry and helpless, and at the same time filled with more power than she had ever known in her life.

Suddenly, Barras's body began to shake, and she drew back, astonished to see that he was laughing.

It was only then that she came to her senses and felt the persistent jerking on the rod she still clutched blindly in her hand, and knew that she had a fish.

"Barras!" she exclaimed in excitement, giving over her immediate attention to the line, "what shall I do?"

Quickly, and without losing his embrace about her, he took the reel in his hands, stoking in the line.

A fine big trout broke the water, hooked on the fly, then plunged beneath the surface again.

"It would seem that you have hooked two fish at once!" he said, laughing. "But my dear, what a beauty *that* one is!"

Eve took back the rod and applied herself to reeling in the trout. Although she would have very much preferred to have Lord Barras kiss her again, she was too much the sportswoman not to feel a thrill of success and pride as she drew her very first fish toward the shore.

"Hold the line tight!" Barras commanded as he descended among the reeds with his net, and Eve, left in charge of rod and reel, did as she was told.

She watched with amusement as Barras waded up to his knees in the stream, skillfully netting the trout, a handsome creature nearly a foot long that flapped with great energy as Barras gripped it firmly and disengaged the hook.

"I say!" he exclaimed, holding it up for her to admire, "not bad at all! Beginner's luck of course, but really not bad at all!"

Eve bit her lower lip. "Beginner's luck!" she demanded. "Nonsense!" She reeled the hook back to her rod and glared at him indignantly, the moment quite gone. "You shall see that I shall quite out-fish you in the end! I wager you would not tell Mrs. Fotherby that she had beginner's luck."

"Mrs. Fotherby would never fish," Barras announced loftily, placing the trout in his creel. "She would consider it entirely unfeminine."

"Then Mrs. Fotherby is a milk-and-water wretch," Eve pronounced. Barras shook his head. Unfortunately, she was occupied with a tangle of line in her reel and did not see his devilish grin.

"Mrs. Fotherby," he announced, "is a mistress of all the virtues a man looks for in a woman."

"Stuff and fudge!" Eve said. "I can just see her, vapouring on a chaise and eating bonbons all day long. I'll wager she keeps a small lap dog with a bow in its hair and a loud, yipping tongue!"

Barras was engaged in carefully scaling the muddy bank, balancing his creel in one arm. "Of course she does; I gave it to her. She named it Joli, as a matter of fact, after me."

"*Joli?* Pretty? But you are not pretty at all," Eve said frankly. "In fact quite the contrary. No one would ever mistake you for an Adonis."

"Nor would anyone mistake you for a civil tongue, my girl!" Barras replied, sliding back in the mud a bit. "Give us a hand, that's a good girl."

Clutching rod and reel, Eve bent down and offered her hand to Barras. "Careful, now," she admonished seriously, "my sister and I were forever coming home muddy and tangled from building mud houses on the stream banks, and they are quite slippery—"

But it was too late; a misplaced step had caused Lord Barras to lose his footing and he began to slide backward, still clutching Eve's hand. His weight, far greater than hers, was enough to cause her to lose her balance, and his grip impelled her toward him as he slid back into the reeds and the water.

Down they both went into the stream, Barras first, landing on his backside with a great splash and a greater shout, Eve tumbling down on top of him.

Lines, reel, rod, creel, skirts and jackets became entangled as Eve slid, against her will, into Barras's wet lap.

Happily, the water was not cold, nor was it deep, and as she came up, sputtering water and gasping for air, she found herself caught up in his protective embrace, their faces no more than an inch apart.

This time, she could not read the expression she saw in the depths of those dark eyes, but some instinct made her uneasy, as if she had seen that he had discovered the truth about her identity.

Soaked to the skin from his ducking, Barras's hair hung about his craggy face in strings, and the twist of his lips was not a smile but another expression, like that of a man with a deep hunger.

Before she could say anything, Barras's fingers had closed tightly about her upper arms and he was drawing her toward him, his eyes half-hooded and his lips parted.

What had come before was a light kiss, Eve realised as she allowed herself to be inexorably drawn to him by those powerful hands. She felt as if she were made of beeswax, melting before the flame of his passion, as if she had no will in the white heat of her craving for his kiss.

Such a surrender was a new experience for Eve Dartwood, but never before had she felt such a strong attraction to a man, nor felt his yearning for her, as intense as the sun of Naples.

They kissed again, and this time Eve found herself responding in kind to him, learning without words from his examples.

This was a closeness she had never before felt, it was like the intimacy she shared with her twin, and yet it felt more intimate, in a way that was different, puzzling, and delicious enough that she never wanted it to end.

There was strength there, but tenderness, too, and she discovered a strength of her own as her arms sought to embrace him almost of their own accord, wanting to touch the place behind his ears, the nape of his neck where his hair fell in golden rivulets, responding with heightened sensation as he played his fingers through her short hair and held her so close to him that she could feel his heart beating through his wet shirt.

When at last he pulled away from her, she was sorry; she wanted the moment to go on forever, a delicious foretaste of the pleasures that awaited her. Well then, perhaps not forever; she wanted more, of course, she thought in dark and confused swirls of feeling, but what she wanted was the *magic* of this moment to go on forever and ever . . . as if she had fallen into a strange dream and never again wanted to wake up from it.

She laid her cheek against Barras's wet white shirt and listened to the beating of his heart in his strong chest, content to hold him and be held by him while the water swirled all around them, moving toward the river and then the sea, sweeping her with it.

"A pretty pair we must be," Barras said, and his voice, rumbling his chest, had lost its cocksure edge. She knew then that he, too, had this feeling, that this was no mere seduction for him, but something grander and larger than both of them, some rare and special connection.

With thumb and forefinger, he lifted her chin so that she was looking at him, and he smiled. "You want me to kiss you again, and believe me, there is nothing more I should like to do at this moment than precisely that. Here, at least, we do not seem to find ourselves in competition." He smiled his twisted grin, but his voice still had a tremor in it that betrayed his emotions. Slowly, he pushed away a lock of wet hair that hung in her eyes, caressing her cheek. He was so close that she could see the golden flecks in the depths of his brown eyes, and the way that his eyebrows grew into questioning, upward streaks. Somehow, she found this endearing, and wanted very much to touch them.

But, as she put out her hand to do so, he caught it within his own, holding it tightly against his rough cheek.

The moment lasted only an instant, and then he was rising from the water, helping her to her feet, his eyes dancing with laughter.

Eve swallowed hard, holding on to his hands. "Barras—Gervase! There is something I *must* tell you—" she began.

Surprisingly, maddeningly, he laughed. At that moment, he looked young, as he must have looked when he was a young boy, just down from Harrow and not yet jaded by title and fortune, reputation and status. "If only you could see yourself right now, soaking wet, with a bit of duck grass wound through your hair like a wreath—you could be an undine, a water sprite, you know!"

Suddenly, Eve was conscious of her thin muslin gown clinging to her body and began, somewhat ineffectually, to pull it away from herself.

"Leave it be!" Barras commanded. "The sun will dry us both out soon enough." And with that, he picked her up in his arms as if she were no more than a rag popper and climbed easily up the bank, depositing her on the warm and sunny grass in the meadow beside the wicker basket Tallant had thoughtfully packed for this expedition.

His jacket lay where he had dropped it carelessly in the reeds and he picked it up and draped it about her shoulders. "This should protect you from me, and from any sudden chills. I don't know which your admirable Miss Fisher would deplore the most, but we shall take no chances. You uncork that bottle of Madeira and let it breathe while I go and see what I can do with this rod and reel. One of my best from Manton, too! You know, my dear, I must hold you in vast affection! I let you drive my team and now I have allowed you to touch my fishing tackle! The next thing you know, you'll be firing my guns!"

"I can do that, too," Eve said happily as she dove into the wicker hamper and withdrew a bottle of wine. She watched as Barras struggled down the bank to retrieve his tackle, and made no comment as he opened the creel and allowed the trout, frightened but unhurt by its brief captivity, to flip out of the straw basket in a shimmering silver arc, suspended in the sunlight for a moment before it hit the water and swam away, gone until another day.

Somehow, she liked him all the more for that single gesture, and turned a deaf and unreproving ear to his curses and imprecations as he sought to untangle his waxed cotton fishing line, sadly balled about the reel and through the reeds.

"I'll have to take this reel apart now," he said, "and oil it all down. No use letting my groom try his hand at it; he's ham-fisted away from horses and a landsman besides. Damn!"

While he played with his recalcitrant tackle, which seemed, as mechanical things frequently do, to have developed a mind of its own, Eve spread the contents of the luncheon hamper on the linen cloth.

"My," she said thoughtfully, "Tallant at least, seems to approve of you. This is a bottle of Papa's ninety-six, and since the war, Tallant has been most particular about doling out the good vintages. And cold chicken and a round of the home farm cheese, and barley seed bread, and the *moutarde à la grecque* that you liked so much at dinner last week, and profiteroles too!"

"I am starved," Barras said, "not having eaten since breakfast. Well, let us feast then, and drink, and hope that we are at least dry enough not to cause comment when and if we return, my water nymph." He pulled off his boots, ruefully watching as he poured water into the grass, and wrung out his socks, hanging them to dry on a bramble bush. His shirt soon followed, and beneath her eyelashes Eve studied the ripple of his muscles and the way in which the sun played on the golden hair on his chest, wondering how one could feel such yearning toward another human being, and at the same time feel so entirely comfortable with him.

She poured him a glass of wine and he tasted it, nodding. "To Tallant, then," he said, "who makes all things possible."

Eve poured her own glass and they toasted.

"Barras, there is something I must tell you," she said at last, swallowing hard. "I cannot allow things to go on like this—"

Lightly his lips brushed hers, and then he lay down on the grass, with his face to the sun, holding up the glass to study the full, rich colour of the grape. "Not before eating," he said lazily. "Never make confessions before or during meals. It ruins the event, you know. My grandfather told me that, and I do believe he was right. The

Georgians were right about a great deal, I am beginning to think, although in my wasted youth I believed them hopelessly old-fashioned. Time enough for confessions after we've buckled. That chicken looks very good! Do you prefer breasts or legs? Breasts, then? Good, for I am a glutton for the leg!"

Eve sighed as she served his plate. Not of a melancholy outlook, and as much inclined to postpone whatever was unpleasant as was her father, she decided that confessions and solutions could wait for the moment to pass.

But she wanted this moment to last forever: this sunlit meadow, this stream, this man, this new happiness she did not deserve.

There was a tiny pinprick of guilt as she thought of Thomas Perry, closed up in the library with poor Amy on such a glorious day. But Barras distracted her immediately.

"Did you ever think," he wondered idly, "that the ancestors of these grapes in this wine were grown by our friends the ancients. Now, you know what Pliny said about wine, don't you, my dear . . ."

Eve did not, but since it came from Barras, she wanted very much to know.

Chapter
Eleven

EVE NEEDED HAVE NO fears that Amy and Thomas were closeted up in the library at Dartwood House on such a fine summer day. As she was gracefully serving Lord Barras his chicken leg with *moutarde à la grecque,* not more than a mile or two away, Miss Amy Dartwood and the poet were indulging in that time-honoured Oxford tradition of punting on the Thames.

That is to say, Mr. Perry, beautifully turned out as always in a pearl grey jacket of broadcloth and a handsome high-crowned beaver, was propelling the flat-bottomed skiff along the current beneath the willow trees that dipped toward the river. Miss Amy lay in the customary reclining position among several cushions in the bow, holding an ivory-handled parasol in one hand while she allowed the other to trail gracefully through the waters.

Mr. Perry, who had an eye for such things, was inclined to think Amy very prettily turned out in a summer toilette of ivory muslin with the most delicate of lavender sprig prints, caught at the waist with a ribbon in the same colour. An ivory spencer of light silk toile protected her décolleté and arms from the injurious rays of the sun, while her piquant, heart-shaped face peered very fetchingly out from beneath the brim of a lavender chip-straw hat festooned with violets and green ribbon. Her sole ornament was a rope of seed pearls, and the tips of her tiny feet, just peering out from beneath the hem of her round gown, betrayed her little sandals of satin ribbon.

It would have been uncharitable to accuse the poet of comparing the sweet simplicity of Miss Amy's style with the more fashionable and dashing tastes of Miss Dartwood, but comparisons between the twins were almost inevitable, even in a mind so finely elevated as Mr. Perry's. Truth to be told, Mr. Perry's discontent with Miss Dartwood's conduct had been rising in almost direct proportion to his satisfaction with the demure and intelligent company of Miss Amy, who even now was delighting him with her ability to recite, in the whole, John Milton's sonnet on his blindness in sombre and affecting tones.

When, upon declaiming the last line, she looked at him with clear green eyes of pure vision, it was all he could do not to abandon the punt to the current and set to composing his own lines upon the refinement of her clear gaze.

That the gentle glow in which Amy had been moving about of late might have been inspired by his presence in her life was something neither of them was ready to contemplate.

Today it had been enough for him to cast aside an inventory of ages past and declare that they deserved a holiday. Amy, whose character was methodical, found this unexpected proposition quite exciting, and upon discovery that the Cambridge-dwelling poet had never experienced punting on the Thames, had suggested that such an expedition would be easily accomplished, as her cousin Timothy, long since called into the Queen's Household Cavalry, kept a punt in the boat house at Seale Abbey.

No holiday is enjoyed quite as much as an unofficial one, and it was with a great deal of merriment that the pair collected their wicker basket from Tallant and made their way across the style to Seale Abbey, feeling like schoolchildren.

Happily for all concerned, their course took them downriver rather than into the trout stream that ran through Seale, and thus the two odd pairs were able to avoid each other's company, or else the events of the day might never have transpired as they did.

A boating expedition was precisely the sort of outing that Amy most enjoyed. It involved neither competition with impatient partners nor violent exercise at which she would soon tire, and best of all, there was no letting of blood or any other sort of rural unpleasantness attached to it. One simply allowed oneself to be carried along through the high banks and the drooping willows at the most leisurely of paces, well able to admire the green of the countryside and the summer wildflowers in bloom.

Nothing could have been more solicitous of her comfort than Mr. Perry's attitude as he piled cushions behind her back and worried that she might become in the least damp from the hull of the boat, tenderly spreading blankets beneath her and opening her parasol lest she be too frail to even attempt that action.

He had handed her into the boat as if she were made of cotton wool, and had watched over her welfare so tenderly that she felt none of her usual qualms about tipping out or running aground on a snag, as she had before when out on the water with her cousin or her sister. Instead she was able to relax and enjoy the voyage.

"'*Doth God exact day labour, light denied?*'" Amy repeated thoughtfully, feeling the cool water flowing around her hand as it trailed through the dark green waters.

"Milton, yes," Mr. Perry said, quickly recovering himself from his reveries, which had been upon Miss Amy Dartwood and not upon the Puritan Poet. "'Lycidas,' now, I find that a most affecting piece of work, but his 'Paradise Lost,' well, what can you say about an epic where Satan is infinitely more interesting than God?"

"Oh, but evil is always much more *interesting* than good, you know," Amy pointed out, lazily. "Only look at Macbeth, or Shylock, or Lear, well, he doesn't become interesting until he does something thoroughly wicked, like throwing that poor girl out into the cold."

Thomas laughed. He saw her point. "Did you know that I once considered taking Orders?" he asked. "My father was a bishop, you know."

"No, I didn't know that," Amy replied, much interested. "But of course, I can see it, you know. You are so naturally good." She clapped her hand over her mouth, but Thomas merely laughed.

"And Barras, being evil, is much more interesting, it would seem. To your sister, at any rate." His tone was matter-of-fact and thoughtful, but Amy still felt a twinge of discomfort.

"Oh, no! Not at all! I am sure that she is most loyal to you, Thomas, it is only that she must dissuade Lord Barras. And, at any rate, I don't think he is evil, precisely. Arrogant, jaded and forthcoming, perhaps, but not evil, certainly."

"Only more interesting than me," Mr. Perry repeated.

"I would not say so! Never! Why, you are made of spirit, while he is quite flesh. Sometimes I think he might be a little decadent, you know, something of a loose fish," Amy confided naively.

Mr. Perry's lips twitched, but he did not laugh aloud, not wishing to hurt Amy's sensibilities, which he found delightful. "Very much a loose fish, I fear," he said. "He leads a most fashionable life in London, you know, and is well known in all the clubs."

To both of them, the fashionable life of the metropolis was somehow synonymous with vaguely sinister sophistication, and they exchanged a meaningful look.

"Which," Mr. Perry quickly added, his conscience stricken, "is not to say that the fellow isn't top-of-the-trees, because there's no saying that he is not. He's very good company, you know, and has a wonderful knowledge of antiquities. Couldn't ask for a more regular sort of a man, but a bit too much of a Corinthian for me."

"Lord Barras is very much the sporting gentleman," Amy agreed.

"Exactly so! He wouldn't do for you at all! Always on the go, always out at a mill or a turn-up, driving to an inch, riding to hounds, fishing, gunning, that sort of thing. I daresay it's all very well and good for Eve, for she likes that sort of thing, but for you, Miss Amy, I should choose a more quiet, more spiritual sort of gentleman."

Beneath the brim of her hat, Amy's milk-white skin turned a bright scarlet, and she lowered her parasol to cover her blushes.

It was several moments before she trusted herself to speak, and when she did, it was only because she was certain that he could hear the pounding of her heart from the stern of the punt, so loud did it seem to her. She knew with all her certain heart that it was very wrong to encourage this line of conversation, and yet, at the same time, she could not stop herself. It was as if some dormant imp within her soul had come to life and now guided her reckless tongue.

"And what sort of a man would you suggest he would be? That is, *who* would that gentleman be?" She could have bitten her tongue, so angry was she with herself. Always, always when she wanted to be able to speak elegantly and cleverly, she found herself *aux anges*, tongue-tied and bound with her shyness. How much she hated her retiring nature, how much she wished that she were witty and clever! But she was not, and she knew it, and that was that. She felt her cheeks burning and wished she could bury her face in the cushions.

But Thomas did not seem to notice, or even to share her sentiments on her shyness. "Perhaps—if you would forgive me for saying so, Miss Amy, a man like me," he offered with sudden passion.

She looked up.

Their eyes met across the boat.

"Oh, Thomas," Amy said simply, "you, too?"

He could only nod.

A boatload of undergraduates from the university passed them by, full of wine and music and happiness, but they might have been ghosts from the Middle Ages for all that Thomas Perry and Amy Dartwood noticed them; they could only stare dumbly at each other, pinioned into shocked and stunned silence by this mutual confession of feeling.

It was only when their punt had drifted into the lane of the undergraduates' skiff and one of the fellows called "I say, sir, dead ahead!" that Thomas recovered himself enough to seize control again and set the boat right upon her course.

When he spoke at last, his voice seemed to come from a great distance. "Do you mean what you say? Do not try to please me, Miss Amy, I could not bear it if I thought you were only being kind."

"Being kind? Oh, no! That is—all these weeks, being with you day after day, in quiet harmony at work . . . that first night in the garden when you mistook me for my twin—" Frustrated, she bit her lip, then tore off her hat. "Why," she exclaimed with unaccustomed spirit, "is it that whenever I want to say something, I fall all over my tongue? It is unfair! Thomas, I think you are the most wonderful man I have ever met in my life! You are good and gentle and learned and kind and patient and—oh, to think that my favourite poet should be saying such things to me! It is more happiness than I deserve!"

"And more happiness than I can bestow!" Mr. Perry said with a sigh. "I would rather rip my tongue from my mouth than to have said such things t'you, when I am not free to—your sister!"

"Yes," Amy said, "my sister. Oh, it would kill her— and she being so kind to me, and suffering so much on my account."

"She does not suffer at all, if you ask me," Mr. Perry remarked. "If you were to ask me, she and Lord Barras seem to be enjoying themselves very much."

"Oh, dear," Amy said, much distressed. She pulled her hat down over her hair again and gazed upon Mr. Perry with wide eyes. "You do not think—"

"I do not know what to think! All I know is that in Italy, I fell in love with one female, only to find that when I returned home, she was but the shadow of the female I truly loved!"

"Aunt Seale says odd things happen to the English when they go abroad, particularly when they go on the Italianate tours," Amy offered.

Thomas threw back his head and laughed. He was handsome, with the sunlight beating down upon him. "Dearest, dearest Amy, you have such a way of placing everything into its proper perspective, you know."

"What did I say?" she asked naively.

"That strange things happen to Englishmen abroad. Bloody awful abroad, it seduces one with sunshine and warmth into behaving as one should not and then when one comes home and is restored to one's senses, well, you do see what happens, don't you?"

But Amy did not understand at all. She had not been, after all, abroad.

"Adorable innocent!" Mr. Perry exclaimed. "But, to know that my feelings are returned—this is bliss indeed."

"But what sad bliss," Amy cried, much agitated. "My sister! Oh, what will she think of me, after she has made such sacrifices upon my behalf? Never, ever did I think that I would—oh, dear!" She looked very close to tears.

"There now," Mr. Perry made a movement as if he would come back to embrace and comfort her, but the punt tilted so much that he was dissuaded from his purpose. "If only I could embrace you now, I would!" he called, poling somewhat unsteadily.

They looked at each other across the space between them, which could have been no more than five or six feet, as if it were the space of some vast American desert. Both romantics, they found this tragedy highly affecting, and, perhaps, just a little satisfying, with all of its dramatic elements of betrayal, confusion, and, at the moment, utter hopelessness.

However, that same pragmatism that had saved Mr.

Perry from the unhappy fate of the *poète maudit* and had made him a most successful Cambridgian don, asserted itself before Amy could make a watering pot of herself.

"There must be a solution!" he declared. "It is simply that we have not yet found it. Aristotle, I believe it was, said that life is but a series of problems that we must solve."

The spires of Oxford, grey stone and medieval, had just begun to move into view over the verdant landscape's trees, and, distracted momentarily from his pursuit of love, Mr. Perry gestured toward them with his free hand. "So beautifully do they sit in the landscape, those turrets of Oxford, hard and dark, so different from the red and gold light of Cambridge," he remarked.

Amy, immediately distracted, dug into her reticule for a pencil and a notebook to note these lines. She may not have possessed a great deal of commonsense, but she knew the beginning of a poem when she heard it coming. Still, as she scribbled, she sniffed loudly.

"There now, there," Mr. Perry called comfortingly. "Please, do not cry, I cannot bear it, to be the cause of your unhappiness, my dearest Amy."

She turned watery eyes toward him, huge and green and very appealing. "But you are the cause of all my happiness, too!" she exclaimed, and then, most inappropriately, giggled. "Do you know what Miss Fisher would say? Miss Fisher would say, 'There now, what you two need to do is eat your lunch. One always feels better after one has had a bite to eat. It feeds the brain.'"

"Miss Fisher is a most admirable female, and I shall always be grateful that you fell beneath her teachings. How dreadful it would be if you were unread and unintelligent, without a thought in your head but horses and parties."

Since this description was perilously close to Eve Dartwood, Amy bit her lower lip.

Mr. Perry had begun to work the punt closer to shore, for he had spotted a place where the willow trees, bending down to the river's edge, formed a sort of bower that would be perfect for an alfresco luncheon.

For several moments he was occupied with this task, and with that of securing the punt in a perfectly steady fashion so that he could move forward to sit beside Amy and the wicker hamper without throwing them all into the water.

In spite of his handsome form, he was not by nature an athletic sort of gentleman, so this took several moments, during which Amy, for lack of any other occupation than self-recriminations over this betrayal of her beloved sister, opened the basket and discovered an identical feast to that even then being consumed by Lord Barras and Eve Dartwood several miles away.

"This is more like it," Mr. Perry said as he settled in on the cushions beside Miss Amy. "Here, let me do that—you would not have the strength to pull a cork from a bottle of wine, my dearest," he advised, taking the bottle of '96 Madeira from her fingers and expertly extracting its cork, which he waved beneath his nose, inhaling the scent. "Good man, Tallant," he said, pouring two glasses of the vintage. "Ninety-six was a good year for Madeira, if for little else."

He handed a glass to Amy, having sampled the vintage and found it precisely to his taste. "To us," he proposed.

"I cannot drink to that," Amy shook her head. "All I can think about is Eve, and what she would feel if she knew about us."

"Eve," Mr. Perry repeated thoughtfully, peering out from beneath the curtain of the sheltering willows into the Thames, where a brightly painted barge boat was making its way up river. All the world seemed to be in a holiday mood. "When I first saw her, at Lady Hamilton's rout ball, in Naples, I found her attractive. It is true, I must admit, that there was a certain rather deplorable levity and irreverence in her conduct that I could not like—you will forgive me for speaking frankly, will you not?"

"Eve is not perfect, and now I find myself to be even less so! What a miserable traitor I am!"

"Hush, hush," Thomas said gently, placing his hand over Amy's. "You are no traitor—the heart has its reasons, and we may never comprehend in our lifetimes, in all our years, what those reasons may be, and yet they compel us, they rule us, they—they make fools of our every sensibility. And yet, they are, and there is nought we can do to escape them. This is our destiny."

Amy stared up at him in open admiration, quite smitten with his expositions of philosophy. Mr. Perry would have been less than human had he not basked in her admiration, recollecting that Eve would have been yawning and changing the subject under similar circumstances.

"Our courtship was brief—we had known each other for barely a week. Yet, I believed, since my admiration for Sir August was so great, that his daughter must be all that I wanted or desired in a bride, and that given time and placed under less, shall we say, saturnalian influences than those in Naples, she would improve her mind and lose, I hoped, some of that sportiveness that I found so decidedly unfeminine in her, and that Lord Barras seems to so strongly admire. Oh, I must say that Eve is a grand sort of female, and a wonderous lady, and that at nine-and-twenty, I realised it was time that I be thinking of marriage. And there is something devilishly intoxicating about Naples—the sunshine and the flowers, the *Lazzaroni* in their bright costumes, the tone set at the court of Ferdinand and Maria Carolina—well, it is one long masked ball, to say the very least! A perfect atmosphere for a young man and a young woman to believe themselves attached, as I am certain that Eve would agree. But when I saw you on that first night of my return to England, sitting in the garden with your guitar, under a full moon, I believed somehow that you were Eve, and that you had become the woman I have always dreamed of. It was only when I discovered that you were you that I realised that for me, Eve was a shade, a shadow of the woman I have waited all my life to meet. In short, Amy, you!"

She opened her mouth to protest, but Mr. Perry, carried away perhaps by wine and his own poetry, forestalled this by leaning over and gently placing his lips against her own.

His breath was as light as air, and his kiss tasted sweetly of the wine he had drunk, as soft and gentle as the little wind that stirred through the willow branches. Slowly and softly, he brushed his lips against hers, and Amy was pleased to find that moonlight madness had not been an illusion at all, and that she was every much enjoying this second taste of the poet's gentle spooning.

Sensibility, so long suppressed, began to open in her soul like a blooming rose, and as Mr. Perry's arms moved softly about her shoulders, drawing her closer to him, her own arms seemed to move of their own accord about his neck, bringing his face into closer contact with her own.

This, then, was what lovemaking was all about, Amy thought, not rough caresses and brutal strength, but tenderness and soft embraces, a sweet yearning that left her feeling almost breathless, and yet protected so strongly within his arms that she might have stayed there forever.

"Dearest, dearest Amy, so fragile and delicate," Mr. Perry said in her ear, and Amy found this to be quite pleasing when compared with the rough things Lord Barras had said when he had tried to kiss her. "You are so small in my arms that I almost fear that I might break you."

She gave a little giggle. "Oh, no, I won't break, please!"

Thomas laughed into her hair, stroking the bright-as-fire curls with his fingers, feeling them wrap about his hand. "Dearest, dearest girl. You are the moon and I am the sun," he whispered, "without you, I am nothing."

"Oh, Thomas," Amy said with a sigh, and pressed her cheek against the warm strength of his dove-grey waistcoat.

"I should like to build you a little house of willow trees, so that we could always live by the riverbank in our little bower," he continued on, his muse catching fire. "We could live like sprites and kelpies on the banks of the river, and sustain ourselves on love alone."

Amy sighed and closed her eyes, relishing the sensation of giving herself over into his embrace. Thomas, looking down at her nestled against his breast, settled against the cushions and smiled, feeling very manly and protective as he enclosed her in his arms.

"If only . . ." she whispered. "If only . . ."

"There *must* be a way!" he said, feeling much less confidence than his tone of voice would indicate. "Never fear, we shall find it. Love," he announced, with the utter conviction of the romantic, "*always* finds a way!"

"I know that we will, but oh, the thought of hurting Eve in any way—I could not live with that, you know. I could never live with that! All of our lives, she has looked out for me, you see, and if I were to steal you away from her—it would be so wrong, so very wrong that I would never live with myself, not ever again."

"Do not think such dark and gloomy thoughts," Thomas replied, although his conscience pricked at him, as a man of honour. "Eve and I are not formally betrothed, you know. We thought to wait until we had returned to England—once she sees, once she understands—"

"I cannot! I cannot! My own sister, with whom I have been closer than any other person on earth—"

"Yes, yes, I understand! Between twins there must always be that bond, Eve spoke of it, too. But, my dearest Amy, there must come a time when you two separate, when you become two different people—"

"I believe it happened when Eve went away to Naples with Papa," Amy said thoughtfully. "Did you know that we had never been apart for more than a few days before that? All our lives, it had been as if we were one person living in two bodies until then. Aunt Seale you know, brought us out in London, and went into fits of despair because it seemed that not only were we doomed by our dreadful carroty, gingery hair, but that no gentleman could seem to separate us!"

"Beautiful, beautiful hair, the colour of sunsets and flame, the colour of ancient gold, the colour of life!" Mr. Perry corrected her fondly.

"But you do see, don't you? It wasn't until Eve went to Italy and I had the influenza that we were apart—for a full eighteen months, nearly two years. And in that time, we grew apart; we have become separate people at last, and not just the Dartwood twins. Aunt Seale used to worry, you know, that we would end up an eccentric pair of old maids, ape leaders, you know, like the Ladies of Llangollen—"

"Not *quite* like the Ladies of Llangollen, I should hope!" Thomas said, laughing. "Adorable innocent!"

"Well, not quite, but you know, that we would be old and eccentric and strange and unmarried, and with only a little money between us, reduced to living in shabby, genteel poverty!"

"My fortune is not as warm as that of Lord Barras, who I am told, is a veritable Nabob, but it is not so small that we should be reduced to living in some shabby, genteel nip-cheese way! I may offer you all the comforts of life, and perhaps even some of its luxuries, but I fear that my house is sadly lacking in grand salons and queen's bedchambers—it lacks even a portrait gallery and a ghost, which I have been told are two of the principal attractions of Highgrove—"

Amy squirmed until she had fitted herself more comfortably to Thomas's form. "Silly man! I don't want all of those things! Don't you see? I am no more fitted to be a viscountess and the hostess of a great household than I am to fly! A small house, a tidy staff, Cambridge—that would suit me very well! There is nothing I should like more than to be the wife of a poet and a don! I hate large parties and I hate grand events, and I am shy with strangers and I fear that Aunt Seale was right when she said I was turning into a wretched bluestocking!"

"I can think of nothing I should enjoy more than an intelligent, well-read and well-mannered wife who would be a comfort to me in every way, and who knows precisely what I like—my own home, my own fireside and my pipe and slippers of an evening, my books and your music . . . oh, Amy, my dearest, my love, how close to heaven it would be to look up from my work and to see you there beside me, to hear the sound of your voice, a more beautiful music to my ears than anything ever composed—"

"It would be a beautiful dream," Amy replied, "if only . . ."

"If only," Thomas repeated. "Yes."

Try as he might, he could not picture Eve performing such routine domestic chores, nor being content in a seven-room house in Cambridge High. Would it break her heart, he wondered, if he were to cry off? Worse, would it break Amy's heart if he were to go through with his arrangement with her sister? Either thought was dreadful to a man of his principles. But the thought of a life without Amy was unbearable to his romantic soul.

He downed the rest of his wine thoughtfully. By God, there must be a way out of this for all concerned. But what would it be?

Try as he might, he could think of no answer.

But, gazing down at his beloved, he felt an odd confidence that he would somehow find one, somewhere.

"Perhaps," he said, without much appetite, but a certain feeling that he must look after Amy, "we should sample whatever culinary treasures Tallant has seen fit to pack for us."

"Yes," Amy said listlessly.

He squeezed her tightly against him, rallying her in hearty tones. "Come now, my dearest! Have a little faith in love!"

Chapter
Twelve

MR. TALLANT FANCIED HE ruled his domains with a firm but fair hand, but Jane Gutherie, the Dartwood twins' maid, had not been in service with the family since the girls come-out without knowing how to manage her superior.

"You mark my words, Mr. Tallant," she remarked, her flashing needle darting in and out of a rent in a riding habit she was mending on the work table belowstairs. "The twins are up to something. Both of them so particular about their clothes, and now I see Miss Amy wearin' all those fine dresses Miss Eve brought back from the Eye-talians with her, and Miss Eve wearing Miss Amy's gowns run up by Mrs. Eisley in the village. You don't suppose they're doing something to fool that pair of gentlemen, do you?" She bent her head to her work so she would not have to meet Mr. Tallant's disapproving eye, and calmly awaited further developments.

"It is not our place to speculate upon the doings of the family," Mr. Tallant pronounced, as he always did when invited to gossip. And then, after a moment, when Jane made no reply, he laid aside the account books and brought out his snuff box. "However," he said, just as she had known that he would, "having been in service at Dartwood House since Sir August was a young man, I can tell you that as children, they were very prone to playing the sort of jests that involved exchanging identities."

Jane nodded her head, holding out her work to examine it from a distance. "It just doesn't make any sense to me, that's all," she said darkly.

Her patience was rewarded when, after a moment's thought and an inhalation and expiration of Old Bureau and some work with his handkerchief, Mr. Tallant said in deceptively casual tones, "Whatever do you mean, Jane?"

"Well," she said slowly, "Miss Eve is ever so much rougher on her things than Miss Amy, you know, and Miss Amy is just a hair smaller than Miss Eve. A maid can tell these things, you know, and I can tell that Miss Eve has been wearing Miss Amy's things and vice-versa, which they never did so since I came into service with them. Oh, there would be the occasional borrowing, a necklace here, a scarf there, and I won't say that if Miss Eve liked somethin Miss Amy had or t'other way round, there wouldn't be a bit of filching things back and forth, and me having to put things to rights again, which I can tell you isn't easy with Miss Eve. Careless, she is, careless with her things, and Miss Amy so careful. Why, the old dress she came home in yesterday from that fishing trip was muddy and damp—and how I am to get those muddy stains out,

I don't know, I will tell you. But it leads me to wonder if they ain't playing some prank on the gentlemen, if you get my meaning."

"Prank? Who's playing a prank, then?" Mrs. Beckley, the cook, wandered in from the kitchen, wiping her hands on a linen towel before settling herself with a gusty sigh into her favourite chair by the hearth.

Mr. Tallant shot Jane a look, as if to say, well, now, you see what you have started. Jane, who knew she was young and attractive, because Lord Barras's groom was forever telling her so, smiled at him angelically.

"Jane has been speculating that Miss Eve and Miss Amy are up to their old tricks," Tallant said with a sigh, picking up his pen again and hooking his spectacles over his ears, as if by this signal he could exclude himself from the conversation.

Mrs. Beckley fanned herself. "Lord, I wouldn't be one bit surprised, although you might have thought they would have grown out of that nonsense by now," she said fondly. "I used to tell them, I used to say, 'I don't care which of you is which, you may each have two macaroons apiece and no more, for it will spoil your dinner. Fair is fair!' Oh, Lord, it is hot in that kitchen! Hot everywhere today, and me with three courses and a remove to get up for dinner and the fish sent up from Oxford about to turn." She waved her linen towel for a moment and then, collecting herself, asked casually, "Now what in the world would them two be up to their old tricks for this time? It seems to me that with those two finally having found a nice pair of gentlemen ready and bursting to pop the question, they'd finally be growing up a little bit, rather than acting like a pair of school girls. When Lady Seale comes back, she should be as pleased as punch, for heaven only knows she's tried hard enough to find them suitable matches. That nice Lord Barras and Miss Eve, for instance, seem suited in every way, and as to Mr. Perry and Miss Amy, well, there's no way around that; the pair of them smell of April and May."

Both Jane and Mr. Tallant looked at her at once. It was Mr. Tallant who spoke first. "Oh, no, no, no, my dear Mrs. B, you've gotten it topsy-turvy."

"It's Miss Eve and Mr. Perry and Miss Amy and Lord Barras."

Mrs. Beckley shook her head so firmly the ruffle on her cap shook, as did several of her chins. "Oh, no, my dears, it's you that have it all wrong. It's Miss Eve and my lord, and Miss Amy and the poet. I may just be a poor simple countrywoman, but I'm not a great booby, not yet!"

"Mrs. Beckley, you are one of the greatest cooks in the Cotswolds, and no one would ever accuse you of being a great booby, but it's t'other way around!" Jane said, much amused. "Of course, you don't see 'em every day, as I do, or as Mr. Tallant does. Even after Miss Eve cut off her hair, I knew who was who by their clothes."

"Well, that may be as it may be, but I could tell you that it wasn't Miss Amy who ate my *moutarde à la grecque* t'other day, because Miss Amy can't abide anything with mustard in it; she never could, not even when she was in leading strings, while Miss Eve can't get enough of the stuff. Have you ever noticed that she spreads it on everything? When you come to me, Mr. Tallant, and said put together a pair of picnic hampers for the young ladies and their beaux, didn't I say *this to Miss Eve and this one to Miss Amy,* and to be careful which got which?"

"Yes, and I did as you requested. I even added a bottle of the good ninety-six to each basket, for heaven knows, I would not want either gentleman to think that I was lacking in any consideration of vintages, especially when we all have such high hopes of a happy conclusion—but what?"

Mrs. Beckley folded her hands across her middle. "Well, there you have it. Miss Eve says to me, everything was good, Mrs. B, but the *moutarde à la grecque* didn't have enough mustard, and Miss Amy didn't touch hers at all, and said Mr. Perry preferred the mayonnaise dressing I made."

Having made her point, she nodded.

Mr. Tallant and Jane looked dubious for a second, then both spoke at once.

"It would fit in with the clothes—"

"Miss Eve has never been a one to stay indoors when the weather's taken a fine spell, such as it has—"

"Well, there you have it," Mrs. Beckley said complacently. "It's Miss Amy and the poet and Miss Eve and the lord. And a fine pair of matches as you could ever wish for," she concluded firmly.

"But Mr. Perry thinks Miss Eve is Miss Amy and Lord Barras thinks Miss Amy is Miss Eve," Jane mused, genuinely puzzled.

"Miss Fisher can tell 'em apart!" Mrs. Beckley said. "Always could."

"But she—she has seemed a little apprehensive of late," Tallant mused. "I wonder . . ."

"Not Miss Fisher! As prim and proper as she is, she'd never, ever lend herself to something like that!" Jane exclaimed, much shocked at the thought. "A proper high stickler, she is, and a governess besides!"

Tallant shook his head. "It all comes," he said gloomily, "of Sir August's being so naffy-minded. The times I've called him to dinner, and had to go and call him again and again because he was lost in some old document or involved with one of those nasty old antiquities. A fine gentleman, Sir August, but as absentminded as any of the dons he's forever inviting to dinner. The old gentleman was like that too, only his particular passion was Roman ruins. May as well have lived in a dream world."

"Or in ancient Britain, the pair of them. Oh, I could have set porridge in for dinner every night and never would Sir August have noticed—his nose would always be buried in a book," Mrs. Beckley remarked. "It's no wonder those two girls grew up as they did, with no steadying influence of a real mother about, God rest her soul, poor Lady Dartwood. Lovely she was, too, with that coppery hair, and knew her house minding too; there was a lady you could cook for, her menus were so nice every day. Poor girls! Well, whatever they're up to, I hope it all works out right and tight in the end, for it's as plain as a pikestaff that it's Miss Amy for the poet and Miss Eve for the lord and not other way round."

"I wonder what the lord and the poet think, then," Jane remarked.

"You are not paid to think, Miss," Tallant said reprovingly. "The affairs of this household are not our business."

"Men!" Mrs. Beckley said, with a wink at Jane over Tallant's bent head.

There was a loud crash from the kitchen, and someone shrieked. Mrs. Beckley sighed. "Drat that girl, what's she done now? If that was my rennet bowl she's just broken, I'll tan her hide!" With an enormous sigh, she shifted herself out of the chair and waddled toward the kitchen.

"Well," Jane said after a moment, "I think it's perfectly odd, that one should pretend to be the other."

"And I think it's none of your business, Miss

Gutherie! You are paid to look after the ladies' clothes, not to speculate upon their personal lives," Mr. Tallant said without looking up from his ledgers.

Jane thrust out her tongue at him, but only when she was certain that he could not see her for the accounts of John Burke & Sons, Greengrocers, the High, Oxford.

When she thought she had waited long enough, she thrust her needle neatly into her pincushion and picked up a pair of Eve's—or was it Amy's—riding boots.

"I think I'll find if the stable has any saddle soap for these. Nasty gash she's laid into the side of them," she said airily as she made toward the kitchen garden door. But she need not have bothered. Mr. Tallant, peering over his spectacles, was muttering to himself about how a man would have the gall to charge ten and six for a bushel of peaches in season.

Lord Barras's groom was precisely where Jane had expected to find him, lounging in the tack room with the Dartwood House head groom, indulging in a half pint of the estate home-brewed.

When he saw her coming, he made some excuse and met her halfway across the stable yard.

"John," Jane said, "D'you recall what I was telling you about Miss Eve and Miss Amy? Well . . ." she took a deep breath and plunged ahead.

Chapter Thirteen

AMY SAT AT HER dressing table, her silver-backed hairbrush idle in her hand. She stared, not at her own reflection in the mirror, but out the window beside it. Her gaze was not upon the rose gardens, nor the Italianate fountains, nor even the home farm of Seale Abbey spread out across the rolling hills beyond. Rather, it seemed as if it were directed inward, for her expression was pensive and grave, and her clear green eyes were unfocused.

Since her return from her expedition with Thomas, she had been more than ever quiet, thoughtful, and almost listless. Miss Fisher, not unnaturally concerned, had begun to wonder if she were suffering from a relapse of the influenza, a question to which Amy had responded with uncharacteristic abruptness and unwonted vehemence as she fled to her room, slamming the door behind her.

She was by nature a moral person. All of her life, she had been guided by the standards of honour and gentility, and by a firm sense of what was right and what was wrong. But now, she was thrown into confusion, as much by guilt as by her own feelings.

There was no denying that what Amy felt for Mr. Perry was an absolute clear and shining love. Although this particular malady had never before affected her in her life, once she had experienced it, she knew it for what it was, and knew that if she did not have Mr. Perry, there was no other man in this life for her. She was past her adolescence, and recognised that the moonstruck passions she had developed at various stages of her career were calf love, such as any adolescent might experience. Her tremendous yearning, at fourteen, for instance, had been for a particularly handsome footman named Charles, who had left Dartwood service to take a position in a London household and had almost broken her heart without ever knowing how much she dreamed of him. At sixteen, there had been Mr. Balderson, a red-faced hunting curate with a most beautiful singing and sermonizing voice, but he, too, had passed on to better things and a plump and comfortable squire's daughter who brought with her dowry the handsome living of East Puddling. In her first London Season, she had thought she might die of aching after a sulky French émigré with a tragic history and smouldering black eyes, but, alas, with French pragmatism, he had elected to return to France when Bonaparte invited a return of the *ancien régime* titles; besides that, whenever she was in his presence, she had become so shy and tongue-tied that he doubtless had believed her to be the next thing to a village idiot.

The dreadful thing was that all these men seemed to have sensed her attraction to them, but had somehow or other taken a look at her and immediately transferred their interests to Eve, who was so much more lively and outgoing. Fortunately or unfortunately, Eve had not the slightest interest in any of them. Well, Amy was not entirely certain she had not almost caught her sister kissing the handsome footman Charles in the backstairs passage, but that did not count.

Eve's school-girl mooning had run along parallel pathways to Amy's. Amy smiled as she recalled her sister brooding over such various males as the undergroom at Seale Abbey, their dancing master. *Really!* And with three children and a sad-looking wife, that was a hopeless case, too! And in London, there had been that spent-out Irish earl, the one with the eye patch and the huge gaming debts who was in search of an heiress to replenish his depleted coffers. Of course, even if Eve had been an heiress, there was still the question of religion, which Aunt Seale was quite firm about, and that had rather knocked out the émigré of the smouldering eyes, too, come to think of it. Really, it was a great pity to come from a family with so many branches in the clergy *and* Aunt Seale, too.

But in spite of the hours, their long, aching, idle hours spent waiting to grow up, to come out and allow their real lives to begin, no one had really ever separated their twin sense.

Eve would and could ache quite as much for Amy's unrequited passions as her own, as did Amy for Eve's, and now she had to smile in spite of herself, recalling the times when they should have been applying themselves to their studies or their needlework or studying their sermon texts for Sunday, when they had woven between them fabulous and fantastic scenarios involving their latest lights of love.

Charles might have been discovered to have been the long-lost son of a rich peer, kidnapped by gypsies as an infant and suddenly and happily restored to his rightful position and fortune so that even Aunt Seale could not disapprove. The dancing master's wife they sinfully pictured in a hundred terrible accidents, with Eve alone able to console her grieving husband. Because of Mr. Balderson's erudition and theology they elevated him to a bishopric (alas, in real life, he was mundane and plodding, and his sermons, while beautifully delivered, were rather dull). The undergroom would migrate to America and return, mysteriously transformed into a gentleman of fortune and ready to claim Eve's hand and whisk her away to live with the red Indians in Philadelphia, in spite of Miss Fisher's best attempts at enlightening geography and economy concerning that city. The French émigré and the dilapidated Irish peer presented something more of a problem, of course, for the twins were older and more sophisticated in the ways of the world by then. But somehow or another, it had been settled that these men would be rehabilitated and made into marriage material. Amy found herself wondering just *how* they had intended to accomplish this, and decided that before they had wrought out some scheme both gentlemen had passed from their lives to greener pastures, leaving behind a pair of forlorn twins and a much-relieved Aunt Seale.

But in the end, they had always had each other, and that was the point, Amy reflected. None of these men ultimately signified because they had always had each other, from the moment of their conception. What real man of flesh and blood could have broken that bond?

It was only accomplished by an accident, by a separation that neither one had planned for, nor actually believed could happen. It was only because they had been apart that she, Amy Dartwood, was finally able to love another human being. At last, she was able to grow up enough to recognise true love when she found it.

Utterly dejected, Amy propped up her chin in her hands on a corner of the delicate mahogany inlaid table. And then, of course, she thought bitterly, the man she had to fall in love with *had* to be her sister's beau!

Thomas had said that there must be a way out of this tangle, but Amy could not see it. All she could see was that she had behaved with the utmost dishonour to the one person in the world to whom she owed absolute and utter loyalty, the one person in the world who was closest to her.

After Thomas, of course.

How strange it was to be so happy and so miserable at the same time. Happy because Thomas loved her and she loved him, because together, they could have a wonderful and enriching life. He was everything she had ever dreamed of in a man, everything she had ceased to believe she would ever find. And she was utterly cast down because he was also the man her sister loved.

"Wretch! Wicked, wicked wretch!" she whispered to her reflection in the mirror. "How could you be so wicked?"

He belongs to your sister, and you see how she has sacrificed for you, what she has done for you, and you, you beast, you turn and serve her a turn like this.

But I did not ask for this to happen. It simply did, as natural as breathing.

You could have prevented it, Amy Dartwood. You know you could have stopped him.

But I didn't want to stop him! I wanted him so badly—and he wanted me, too.

He wants you because Eve is out covering for you with Lord Barras, whom you do not want to marry, although he is not so very bad as he once seemed, in Bath, come to think, but still not Thomas. He wants you because you are like Eve, and he cannot have Eve, so he has deluded himself into believing that you are your sister. Only look in your own mirror and you can see Eve's eyes looking back at you. It is really Eve that he loves, and he will come to his senses again when Lord Barras has gone away again.

Having castigated herself with this interior dialogue, Amy watched her reflection as two large tears rolled down her cheeks.

In the general course of things, she felt rather noble when she had done something to put the good of others above herself. That was the right thing to do, and all of her life Amy Dartwood had done the right thing. This was a little moon madness and nothing more.

Although she believed she was doing the right thing now, she felt far from noble as she laid down the silver-backed brush and rose from the dressing table.

For a moment, and a moment only, she gazed yearningly out the window toward Seale Abbey, knowing that *he* was there, but with the spiny resolution very passive people may sometimes have in moments of extreme stress, she walked herself toward her desk and drew out her writing implements.

It was at this desk that she had read all of Eve's breathless letters from Naples and composed her own replies in return. Perhaps that gave her courage to do what she knew she must, as she drew out her notepaper and her sand-shaker and tested the point of her pen. Still, as she dipped it into the inkwell and began to write her note, her hand trembled and a single tear blurred her opening salutation.

Even as Amy's tears mingled with the ink on her page, next door, Eve, too, sat pensive in the twilight.

In moments of stress, she had been wont to chew on the ends of her hair, but now, as she put her hand up, for the hundredth time in the past fortnight she recognised that it was gone, shorn into a mass of soft curls, and for the hundredth time, she missed it dearly.

She did not regret the sacrifice of it; that was not in Eve's style, for she regretted nothing, once she had set it into motion and plunged blindly ahead, but she did cast a rueful look downward at her ragged and bitten nails, rubbing them against her gown.

She was perched in the window seat, and if she had craned a bit out the window and looked to her left, she might have been able to just catch the tip of her sister's profile, gazing as she was gazing, across the gardens of Dartwood House and the fields of the home farm, toward Seale Abbey's grey-stone east facade.

Twin sense was not much in the offing, and indeed, had not been much in evidence since her return from Naples, but like her sister, she was entirely wrapped up in her own problems, and had not had much time or thought to spare for her sister at that moment.

Perhaps it might have been better if she had, for it would have saved them both a great deal of heartache and pain, but a lifetime spent in protecting her twin from life's unpleasantnesses had inured Eve to pouring out her own troubles upon that sweet and helpless head.

She drew up her knees and rested her chin on their surface, unconsciously nibbling at her fingernails as she stared moodily out the window.

She should, she realised, have been the happiest female in the Cotswolds. After so many years alone, she had met a man who was not only her match, but her equal in every way. Who would have thought that arrogant, odious, careless Gervase Barras would have become the man of her dreams? Certainly not Eve Dartwood, who had been prepared to dislike him upon sight, and now, little more than a fortnight later, found herself head-over-heels in love with him.

That he was equally in love with her seemed like utter bliss, she reflected.

Except.

Except she was in love with a man who thought she was her sister.

And, she was already as good as engaged to someone else.

It seemed to her that all of her life she had been looking for love, although the thought of the way in which she used to swoon over the dancing master could still make her smile; and Lord Kilarney with his eye patch, well, that had been a school-girl's infatuation with a swashbuckler, she knew that now.

One of the odd things about being an identical twin was that one was never alone at all. Love, she had heard, was a search for the missing half of oneself, but she had never had that, because her missing half had never been very far away. Until Miss Fisher had arrived to take charge of their education, they had been brought up very much as if they were one person; they had dressed alike, talked alike, and frequently even done the same thing at the same time, like scratching their noses or saying the same words. Until they were well into their teenage years, they had even slept in the same bed, bundled together as if they were still in their mother's womb. What one had, the other had just the same, and each one was treated in precisely the same fashion as the other, without much chance of allowing either one to develop independently.

Was it any wonder that they had enjoyed switching their identities to fool other people? It had been Miss Fisher who had been able to tell them apart at a glance, and dearest Tabby who had set about allowing them the freedom to develop as individuals. If she had come into their lives earlier, Eve reflected grimly, perhaps her job would have been simpler, but it had become a huge undertaking: encouraging each twin to do what she liked best, to dress differently, to each have her own room and her own things. Tabby had wisely allowed them to separate themselves, preparing them for the day when they might live in a country, perhaps a world apart from one another, with someone else who was an entirely different sort of "other half"—a man.

All too easily, Eve could now look back and see that Aunt Seale's worst fears might have been realised, that they might have become so intertwined that no man—or indeed, no other human being—would have been able to separate them, and they just might have ended up a pair of eccentric old spinsters with a thousand pounds a year between them. They might have dwindled into crazy old ladies such as she had seen in London or Naples, gushing childishly over their cats and their parrots and their small yapping lap dogs, dressed in ancient clothes.

Eve gave an involuntary shudder. All too clearly, that was the fate that had been intended for her and for Amy, until by some miracle Gervase had arrived on the scene.

Distracted quite easily by thoughts of the viscount, Eve leaned back against the window frame and sighed, closing her eyes to relive the moment when he had kissed her.

It was a warm evening, and the wind that blew down the valley was soft and moist. It lifted her tendrils of ginger hair away from her face and carried the scent of the Malmaison roses to her nostrils.

But still, in the end, her thoughts brought her round again to the same unhappy tangles: she was pledged, if not downright engaged to another man, and Barras believed she was her sister.

Oh, she had tried to tell him the truth today, really she had. It was just that the truth got all tangled up with him, and then she was afraid that if Gervase knew what sort of prank she had pulled on him, his pride would be such that he would go off and never come back again, and that she could not bear.

"Well," she said aloud, so softly that she could barely hear herself, "I'll just *have* to bear it, won't I?"

When she had met Thomas in Italy, she had not loved him. Nor, she suspected, had he really loved her. What she had seen was a handsome man who would provide her with a way out of becoming an eccentric, twin-ruled spinster. She understood that all too well now, although at the time, it had truly seemed like love, beneath those sunny Italian skies, those luxurious Italian stars. Perhaps it had been Italy itself that she had fallen in love with, and he was simply there, when she was lonely and missing her sister. It had been a whirlwind sort of thing, nights of parties and balls and masquerades during the Carnival season, when it seemed that all of Naples was glowing with a festival spirit and falling in love was the accepted thing to do. Perhaps in Naples, Thomas had seemed less stuffy than he did now, back in England. Less pressured, less—well, prim and proper. As it was, she had been a little annoyed with his unexpected arrival, for it really had thrown her plans off, and truth to tell, she knew right and tight that she had been deliberately avoiding him for the past week or ten days simply because in their last interview, she had felt irked by his attitudes.

Especially when one compared him with Gervase, who was so free and so easy to be with, who liked to be out of doors and always doing things, and not cooped up in a stuffy room all day long looking at boring old books.

She felt a rare stab of guilt at the way in which she had been ruthlessly foisting him off upon Amy all these days, and promised herself that somehow, she would make it all up to her sister.

But then again, if she hadn't been pretending that she was Amy during all this time with Barras, things would have been much less complex.

No one to blame there but herself, Eve reminded herself firmly. You bought the tangle, and now you can't unsort it.

Like her sister, she had been brought up with the strictest sense of right and wrong, and after she had finished brooding over the mess she had made, Eve had also arrived at the conclusion that as unhappy as it might make her, she must do the right thing.

To cry off from an engagement was a terrible thing, and would cause a dreadful scandal, she realised. Lord Barras had not yet proposed, and there was still time to send him away without comment.

That would save Amy, of course, but there was nothing, absolutely nothing she could do to save herself. Dear, patient, kind Thomas, how hurt he would be if she were to cry off with him at this point!

She simply couldn't do that to him. Even if she realised now that she did not love him, she could still do her best to make him a good wife. And then, in time, when Amy came to live with them, she would be a good sister, too. That was what Aunt Seale had taught them; to honour and value their duty above all things. That was what she must do.

Gervase, she realised, would be angry and perhaps puzzled by her decision, but he was too proud to be hurt, and she could not bear to think of how he would wound her with words and looks if he were told that she had been betraying him all this time, pretending to be her sister.

That she could not bear; a life as a loveless bride was far better than that. No doubt he would find consolation with Mrs. Fotherby, she added firmly to herself. And in time, there would be another young lady, perhaps one more suitable and less hoydenish, to become Lady Barras, and she would make him much happier than Eve ever could have.

Eve did not cry; she rarely cried, but she did sigh long and slowly as she slid off the window seat and walked across the room to her desk.

Gnawing at her nails, she wrote: "My Dear Lord Barras, I hope that you will Understand . . ."

The moon was dark and the garden was hot and still in the wee hours of the morning. Only a dim, discontented chirping of some restless bird disturbed the absolute stillness of sleeping Dartwood House.

Like a pair of magnets, they were drawn to the same place. Eve, a shawl wrapped around her nightgown, huddled silently on the bench, betraying no surprise when Amy, pale and wraithlike, drifted over from the terrace to sit beside her, placing her weary hand on her sister's shoulder.

Eve reached around to give her twin a hug. "Couldn't sleep," she said softly.

"I couldn't either," Amy sighed.

Eve tried to put a light note into her voice. Not for the world would she have unburdened such woes upon her sister's frail shoulders, but Amy sensed them anyway, as Eve sensed Amy's, each one mistaking the other's feeling for her own. "You know," Eve said, "all night long, all I could think about was that young Frenchman and the Irish peer, and the dancing master and the curate and the groom and the footman."

"That is what I have been thinking, too," Amy said with a sigh. "Lord, love has made us a pair of fools, hasn't it?" she asked.

Eve shook her head. "Well, at least we'll always have each other," she said.

But to both of them, no matter how much each loved her sister, it seemed like a very small consolation at that moment in time.

Somewhere off in the valley, an owl hooted plaintively and its mate answered.

Chapter
Fourteen

STATE WAS KEPT IN grand style at Seale Abbey whether the dowager was present or not. Indeed, Lady Seale was fond of saying that should the Prince Regent appear in her absence, she trusted he would find no fault with the hospitality of *her* household, for she believed that allowing servants to idle away half-pay holidays while their mistress was elsewhere was a sort of false economy.

It was to be expected that breakfast at Seale Abbey, the only meal of the day taken there by her two house guests, would live up to her exacting standards. Even though my lady remained in London, her presence was much felt, rather like the perfumed scent she wore, Attar of Roses, which permeated every corner.

But she seemed, to her guests at least, to be present

in more than essence: In the dining room, a Gains-borough portrait, full length and done when she was a young bride, loomed down upon the pair of diners in much the same spirit as the lady would have done herself.

Lord Seale, in the fondness of his youth, had fancied his wife to be a beauty, and there were many, many portraits of her, at various stages of her life, scattered throughout the house. The former Miss Dartwood of Dartwood House had not changed all that much in the past forty years, and for a man as sensitive as Mr. Perry, it was somewhat disconcerting to have the feeling that those critical, omnipotent, steely eyes were not only following one through a single chamber, but from one room to another, watching for every *faux pas*. It must be noted that Gervase Barras, a man of far less sensibility, had tossed a towel over the Hayter portrait in his bedchamber and forbidden his valet, under pain of banishment, to remove it.

Unhappily, Seale Abbey, unlike the charming Queen Anne red brick of Dartwood House, was a vast warren indeed, so added upon and remodeled since the days of the monks that two persons might wander quite comfortably through its drafty chambers and towering state rooms, all William Kent furniture and Italianate rococo gilt, without encountering one another for weeks upon end, a state of affairs that suited the late Lord Seale most admirably toward the end of his life, when he had grown less enchanted by and more wary of his wife's managing character. So many rooms, so many portraits, and everywhere one looked, the determined chin and commanding glare of Lady Seale met one's eye, undisguised by Romney or Lawrence or even the obsequious Cosway.

The footmen who laid out the breakfast covers must have been used to it, as was the butler, a large, rather intimidating person who looked more like a marquess *should* have looked than had the late Lord Seale, a rather unprepossessing man.

In spite of the fact that neither Gervase Barras or Thomas Perry were hearty consumers of the first meal of the day, they met each morning at the table in the dining room to be confronted by dishes of kippers, rashers of bacon, whole strings of sausages, loaves of bread, a mountain of muffins and scones, five or six different jams and jellies, brains, steak, cold ham, cold beef, and eggs. Eggs! Poached, fried, scrambled, omletted, soft-boiled, hard-boiled—every style and possibility of the hard-shelled ovum of the domestic fowl was presented daily.

Mr. Perry took coffee and a muffin.

Lord Barras drank tea and ate toast.

Their proximity as housemates had in no way increased their intimacy with each other's emotions, although they enjoyed a civil and mutually respectful relationship. In the late evenings, they were fond of shooting a game or two of billiards beneath an Isabey portrait of their hostess in the room set aside for the purpose, but in the morning, neither gentleman was inclined toward more than a monosyllabic greeting while they imbibed their beverages and perused their separate newspapers, carefully ironed by the footman before being left by their places.

The morning in question was to start no differently from any of the others that had preceded it in the past fortnight; neither gentleman could have forseen that it would have ended upon a most interesting note.

Mr. Perry was already seated at the vast dining-room table built to feed twenty when Lord Barras descended the stairs, and not for the first time was my lord struck by the incongruity of seeing one very well-dressed gentleman all alone with his coffee and bread and *Times* at the vast board.

"Morning," he said as he poured himself a pot of tea, nodding to the two footmen who stood in attendance.

"G'morning, Barras," Mr. Perry's voice floated up from behind his paper.

Barras dropped two lumps of sugar and poured a dash of cream into his cup and unfolded the *Post*, soon losing himself behind the news of the world outside.

"Can't trust that Bonaparte fellow," he said, reaching for his lukewarm toast, standing on the rack by his plate.

"I once had high hopes of him," Mr. Perry replied, reaching around the broadsheet to pick up a muffin and disappearing again. "I see that they have completed the West Indian Docks project in town."

"And about time, too."

No more was heard from either gentleman for some minutes, save the soft rustle of newspaper as a page was turned. "Ha! Listen to this, Barras, you'll find this interesting—'Alexander von Humboldt has almost succeeded in climbing Mount Chimborao in Ecuador, but was turned back by inclement weather and hostile natives!' Ha!"

"Ha, indeed! Didn't think he could do it. Bloody high mountain, that—bad winds and weather, too. Why, when I was—"

At that moment, a footman in the livery of Dartwood House appeared in the doorway, panting and slightly out of breath.

"Miss Dartwood's compliments, sir, Miss Dartwood's compliments, my lord, and would you be pleased to accept a note?" From the pocket of his livery, he withdrew a pair of twin missives, one sealed with green, the other with blue wax, and, bowing, delivered them to the gentlemen at the table.

"What's this?" Barras asked, fishing in his pocket for

a coin to give the man, but Perry had already beaten him to the gesture.

"What the devil—" Lord Barras said, laughing as he scanned his note in Amy's neat, precise handwriting.

"Good Lord," Mr. Perry whispered as he looked at his, in Eve's large childish scrawl, his face draining visibly of colour.

"Wait, wait," Barras said with a laugh. "I think you have mine and I have yours."

Without a word, Mr. Perry tendered his note and accepted the one Lord Barras offered in return. His blue eyes narrowed as he scanned the missive and he half stood up in his chair. "She cannot say so!" he exclaimed involuntarily.

"It would seem that she does, but *pas avant les domestiques,* if you catch my meaning," Barras said calmly. "Well, she *thinks* she does, at any rate, old man, but you know how these things go—or perhaps you don't, in which case I think we really ought to have a long talk about this pair of ginger-haired hoydens—"

"You know?" Mr. Perry asked, stunned.

Lord Barras, carelessly folding his note and thrusting it into his pocket book, nodded his head. Clearly, he was vastly amused; his crooked smile was more lopsided than ever. "How could I not know?" he asked. "That will be all, thank you," he commanded the pair of footmen, who reluctantly withdrew from the room, only to linger beside the keyhole on the door's other side.

"If you mean, Mr. Perry, did I know that Amy was Eve and Eve was Amy, of course I did! I have suspected since the first moment Miss Dartwood attempted to pass herself off as Miss Amy Dartwood! You don't pick up that sort of tan from lying about a sick bed in Bath, you know!"

"And yet you said nothing," Mr. Perry was clearly

stunned. With long and elegant fingers, he neatly folded up his note and tucked it into a section of his notebook for future reference. "I don't think that I perfectly understand, sir!"

"No," Gervase said with unusual gentleness, "I don't think that you do. But I think, and you must correct me if I am wrong, that you are in love with Miss Amy, not with Miss Dartwood. Or so my groom informs me."

Mr. Perry swallowed hard. "That is true. I am in love with Miss Amy. She is a sweet and wonderful female, and in every way the woman I would want to make my wife!"

"I daresay, but it don't signify, because I'm supposed to be engaged to her, y'know. That was why that hoydenish sister of hers was pretending to be her, I think! Miss Amy's liking for me was never great."

"How can you sit there and smile like that!" Mr. Perry exclaimed. "Certainly, every feeling must be outraged by Miss Dartwood—Miss Eve Dartwood's conduct! I know mine is!"

"On the contrary, old man, I find Miss Eve Dartwood to be the most delectable, unique and spirited hoyden it has ever been my misfortune to meet! And what's more, I'm head-over-heels in love with her, so if you're certain that your feelings are settled upon Miss Amy, I wish you very well!"

"You—and Eve? But she—"

"Calls me an odious, odious man? Yes, and it is music to my ears, when it comes from her lips. Think about it, old man, Eve Dartwood and I are suited in every way!"

Mr. Perry nodded, quite seriously. "Yes, I believe you are," he said. "I suppose I should have seen it coming, but I have been so wrapped up in my own affairs that I was blind to yours."

"Then I think that in future we shall deal very well as

brothers-in-law, for that's the sort of relationship I'll like! Not that I ain't fond of Miss Amy, I am, but it is just that I'm in love with Miss Eve, and have been since the minute she waltzed into the room and pulled the wool over my eyes—or tried to!"

"Eve—she is a wonderful woman, full of many virtues, but as my wife—" Mr. Perry shuddered.

"Precisely so! You need a quiet, contemplative woman who will make a warm home for you! I need a woman with fire and spirit, a woman who may drive me mad, but will never, ever bore me! So, you see, we are very well suited with our choices! Now, it seems to me, we must convince our ginger-haired sisters that we are the right fellows for them!"

"Yes, yes, of course! Let us go over to Dartwood House at once!" Mr. Perry exclaimed, much relieved. "I knew there was a solution to all of this, but if I had known that you knew about Eve's deception . . . well, it was very wrong of her, but she meant well. Amy, you see, is not a courageous person."

"And I was too bold for her! But not, I think for my Evelina! Ah, Mr. Perry, what could be better?"

At that moment, the butler lurched into the room, looking very much like a marquess should look.

"Lady Seale!" he announced in resounding tones.

Even had her portraits not hung all over the house, there would have been no mistaking Lady Seale for any other.

Like a man-o'-war under full canvas coming into home port, she sailed majestically into the room, at once dominating it by her sheer physical presence, which was formidable, and made more so by the towering plumes in her hat and the vast white fichu covering her bosom. The scent of Attar of Roses surrounded her as she thrust out a gloved hand toward Lord Barras.

"Dear Gervase! How very good to see you! I trust you have been made comfortable in my absence? Good, excellent," she said, with the confidence of one who knows there is no other way.

Lord Barras and Mr. Perry had risen from the table upon her entrance, and now, with the full force of her gaze turned upon him, Mr. Perry understood what the Dartwood twins meant when they discussed their Aunt Seale. He was a strong man, but he felt at that moment as if he were a grubby school boy again.

"Lady Seale, may I present Mr. Perry?" Barras murmured, and Thomas's hand was gripped firmly within a vice disguised as a York tan glove.

"Yes, yes! How d'ye do, Mr. Perry? So very glad to meet you! And I trust your stay has been pleasant here?"

"Yes ma'am, very pleasant," Mr. Perry said, basking in the sudden and unexpected charm of Lady Seale's brilliant smile, full of large white teeth. She reminded him of the matron in his first form house at Harrow at that moment, and he began to appreciate her.

"Oh, yes, my lady, most pleasant," he said, and she nodded. Heaven help her staff if there had been any complaints!

"I do enjoy masculine company! You know, I must be frank—Gervase will tell you that I always say what is on my mind, I had my doubts about you. A poet, after all! But Sir August assures me that you are exceptionally rational for an artist, and that your father was General Perry, such a very worthy man, so you must be all right!"

"Th-thank you, ma'am!" Mr. Perry managed to say, stunned as he was. "I-I hope so!"

"Oh, indeed," Lady Seale replied blithely, "although of course, one does wonder about Eve as a don's wife, but there you have it!"

Thomas threw a beseeching look at Lord Barras, who was smiling blandly.

"Anyway, it doesn't signify! I purchased a book of your poetry in London, although I have never been much for reading, and I found your work refreshing! None of these nasty words or innuendoes one sees so much of these days, just good solid verse! You must autograph it for me when my maid unpacks it!"

"It would be an honour, ma'am," Mr. Perry said gravely. "Good, solid verse!" he repeated in thoughtful tones.

"Keep up the good work, and you shall go far! I recommended it to one or two of my poetical friends, and you may be certain that I shall do what I can to make you all the rage in fashionable circles!"

Mr. Perry felt as if he had been caught in the wake of that man-o'-war, but he merely nodded.

"Now," Lady Seale said, taking off her gloves and her hat and tossing them on a chair as she sat heavily down at the table, "I have not yet had my breakfast, so I will do so as we talk."

As she spoke, a primly dressed female of uncertain years appeared from nowhere, clucked her tongue as she picked up the hat and gloves and was about to disappear when she was commanded by her mistress to seek out that book of poetry from my lady's baggage. The abigail clucked her tongue again and disappeared, to be replaced by one of the footmen, who began to quickly and silently pour coffee and dish up various comestibles from the covered platters on the sideboard.

"Of course, when I met Sir August in London, he told me all about Mr. Perry, and I thought—"

"Sir August? In London?" Mr. Perry asked.

Lady Seale threw him a look as if to say that anyone who was anyone would know Sir August was in London. "Of course, he put into Portsmouth quite a week ago. The political situation in Naples is not good, again, alas."

"But we have had no word from him, you see—"

Coffee was placed before my lady and she sipped before she answered. "A little more cream, if you please, George! Thank you. I am not surprised, you know, to hear that my brother neglected to inform you of his return! Sadly absentminded, August is! Especially when he is sunk in his studies, as he has been! Why, I was walking down the Brompton Road, and I happened to run into him, else I would never have known he had returned, his own sister! He had left his club and was on his way to the British Museum, and of course ended up on the Brompton Road, as he *will* do when he's abstracted in thought. So, of course he told me that Eve was to be engaged to you, Mr. Perry, and I of course said, well, this is nice, since Amy is engaged to be married to Lord Barras, which he seemed pleased to hear." With a healthy appetite, she dug into a huge platter of eggs and kidneys, oblivious to the look the gentlemen exchanged above her head.

Mr. Perry looked horrified; Lord Barras merely smiled and shrugged.

"So," Lady Seale said around mouthfuls of food, "I immediately got busy. No matter what I had to do in London, I knew that I had to do the right thing by my nieces. My brother is not an attentive parent. Or an attentive anything else, if it don't concern some ancient old fustian Greek or Roman! An excellent man, but not at all on top of things, as I am! In a way it's too bad it's in the middle of the Season, and everyone is in London, but I shall open up the house for the weddings, at least! I know how to do the right thing! But at any rate, I have arranged a very small and very exclusive ball for Seale Abbey on the thirtieth—a week away—in which Sir August can announce the girls' engagements. And I also have alerted the *Post* and made certain the announcements have been placed, and left instructions with Madam Celeste that the girls will be going to her for their gowns! Two trousseaus to get ready! So much to do! But never fear, I am equal to the task and willing to make any sacrifice!"

Relief and anticipation were both in her tone. Perhaps, having despaired of ever marrying off her nieces at all, let alone to a pair of prize catches such as Barras and Mr. Perry, she could be excused her enthusiasm. Never let it be said that Lady Seale was behind in any aspect of social nicety, however; when it came to marking the great ceremonies of life, she knew precisely what to do, and could be counted upon to dispatch it all with great style.

"Lady Seale, I fear that I must tell you—" Mr. Perry began, but Lord Barras, with the nudge of his toe against Mr. Perry's foot, cut him off ruthlessly.

"I am sure that Mr. Perry means to say that we are honoured!" he exclaimed. "Most honoured indeed!"

"Well, I should feel more honoured if Sir August would come home so everything may be finalised," Lady Seale said with a sigh. "You know, settlements and all of that. It is really a great deal too bad that he has been caught by something and wants to linger on in London at the British Museum Reading Room forever and ever! He should be here to attend to these little formalities! However, I daresay it doesn't really signify in the least, because it's all done with the solicitors, isn't it? Not that it isn't so much better that way, but one would wish that my brother were a little more anxious to see these matters attended to! He lives in a world of his own, however, and always has, so it can't be helped."

Lord Barras cleared his throat. "Do the ladies know that you have returned?" he asked.

"No, but they soon shall! I've sent a footman down to Dartwood House to tell them that as soon as I've gotten myself together, we shall sit down and plan! There is so much to do for my little ball, and heaven only knows if Amy has a suitable gown—Eve of course has brought an entire new wardrobe back from Naples with her, but Amy's not the clotheshorse her sister is, and I shall need a hundred and one little things done between now and then, so you gentlemen need not expect to see too much of the females between now and then!" She wagged a finger at them, and smiled her new, white-toothed smile, so different from the one Lord Barras recalled seeing in Bath. He knew then what had kept Lady Seale in London so long. It had not been social engagements, but a trip to her dentist to be outfitted with new teeth, and very handsome, wolfish teeth they were, too. They suited her personality ideally, he thought, and tried to suppress his smile.

"But Lady Seale!" Mr. Perry exclaimed. "You do not perfectly understand how things stand here!"

"What Mr. Perry wants to say is that the ladies seem to have developed a case of, well, cold feet, as one might say."

Lady Seale raised an eyebrow at the vulgarism, but was in such a good mood that she made no comment, prepared to allow this to pass by. "Well, of course! It's only natural, you know! All females do that! Want to be sure they're making the right choice! Why, my cousin Lavinia had to be pried out of her bedroom for her engagement party, and that was a love match! It runs in the family, you know; all the Dartwood women are famous for prenuptial jitters! Just you leave it all to me! I'll bring them about!" She spoke so certainly that neither Mr. Perry nor Lord Barras had the least doubt as to her ability to coerce the Dartwood sisters into *anything*.

"You must be the judge of that, of course," Lord Barras said gravely.

"Of course," Lady Seale said complacently. "Now, I want you two to run along and do something interesting together, for I am sure that the girls will be here soon, and we shall want to discuss female things that would be of no interest to you at all!"

She smiled her new and blinding smile at them.

"The groom," she said, "is of no further interest to us until he presents himself in evening clothes at my ball. And the wedding, of course. The rest is all done by the females and would be a dead bore to you."

"Oh, I think not," Lord Barras murmured. "In fact, I believe it would all be very interesting indeed!"

Lady Seale waved a hand in his direction. "Run along, boys," she said, already ringing for the butler. "I'll take care of everything from here on in!"

"Barras!" Mr. Perry exclaimed, the minute they were out of the house. Lord Barras's phaeton stood hitched and ready in the driveway, and automatically, Thomas swung himself into the perch.

Barras paused for a moment to have a word with his groom, then easily hoisted himself aboard the phaeton. He took up the reins and geed his horses, who came to life in a smart trot.

"Barras," Mr. Perry repeated. "Why didn't you tell Lady Seale what the ladies had written? Can't you see it is all over?"

"Not all over by a long shot, old fella. When the old

trout works on them a bit, they'll come to hand easily enough, you mark my words."

"I cannot—"

"Trust me, Perry. I know what I'm doing."

"Then I am heartily glad one of us does! Barras, what scheme have you in mind? This is ridiculous!"

"Yes, it is ridiculous, I will grant you that. But are you bored?"

"Bored, no! Good Lord! Outraged, indignant, confused, puzzled, yes, but bored, no!"

"Exactly so! I cannot remember the last time I was bored since I fell under the spell of Miss Evelina Dartwood. And before that, well, I was bored all the time. Damned bad thing, boredom!"

"Barras, this deplorable levity is totally inappropriate! Our entire futures hang in the balance, and if things continue on this way, we are both liable to find ourselves married to the wrong twin! A very pretty state of affairs!"

"Sarcasm ain't your forte, Perry. It never works with poets, you know. Rest easy, though, all will come out right in the end!"

"Oh, and I suppose you have a plan," Thomas said, sighing.

Barras grinned at him crookedly. "As a matter of fact, I do! For a minute there, I believed Lady Seale's unexpected arrival would throw a monkey wrench into it, but now I see that it, too, can be worked to our advantage!"

"What advantage? This could not possibly be more tangled! You have received your congé and I, mine. No power on earth will induce those twins to marry us now!"

"Oh, yes it will! You don't know Lady Seale! By God, she almost had me buckled to Amy, and I ain't a weakminded sort of man, not by a long shot! Listen, old man, what say you that we take a drive into Oxford this morning? It's a nice day and it's as plain as a pikestaff that we ain't wanted anywhere in the neighbourhood until things calm down a bit."

"That much is true, but I fail to see what a visit to Oxford could possibly accomplish!"

"One: it will keep us out of the way of Lady Seale, and that should be enough. Two: I need to find Shelldrake, Sir August's man of business. I'll warrant if anyone can rout Sir August out of the British Museum and bring him home from whatever scholarly fit and start he's gotten on now, it would be Mr. Shelldrake. Particularly if I was to tell Sir August's man of business that I was willing to make him a very good offer on the Etruscan goddess I knocked his daughter down for in the Westerby's auction!"

"His daughter? What do you mean? Eve did not—even she could not have attended an auction! A public auction!"

"Relax, old boy, she was done up like a Moslem widow in purdah, all veils and bonnets and disguises. No need to worry that anyone else knew it was her but me, and I wouldn't have known it was her if I hadn't heard her voice again so soon!" He reached over and gave the astonished Thomas Perry a friendly nudge.

"No, old boy, I daresay you're better off without her! She'd send you into fits and starts of your own, and that would never do! A creative sort of a chap ought to have a peaceful home life, if nothing else! No, I think she would be better off with me, truly I do! She may drive me mad, but she will never bore me, and that is more than I can say for any female I've ever met in my entire life!"

"Then you knew all along, but you never said anything about Eve's disgraceful ruse!" Mr. Perry exclaimed.

"That's about right. I wasn't sure at first, of course,

but after about an hour or so, I knew it was true; for some reason Eve was pretending to be Amy and vice-versa. Fool that I am, it took me a great deal longer to discover *why*. You see, I had hoped that if I acted like a dreadful boor, Amy would cry off from the engagement. You've seen Lady Seale! She is a *very* managing woman! The moment she saw in which direction I was headed in Bath, it was as if I were already leg-shackled to her niece. Well, I am of an age where I ought to marry, you know, and I have nothing against the institution itself, and there is the matter of an heir, but—well, I wasn't entirely certain Amy was the girl for me. I had hoped to give her such a disgust of my character that she would cry off when I came into the Cotswolds. But she didn't. Eve did! And right away, I knew this was the woman for me! And that beautiful ginger hair, too! But then, you know about ginger hair—we seem to share a taste for that!"

"The light begins to dawn," Mr. Perry said. "But you were so intent upon dangling your mistress in front of her—but then that would explain it all!"

Mrs. Fotherby? Regrettably, there is not, nor was there ever, a Mrs. Fotherby. That was an invention of my own to drive Miss Eve even wilder than she already was. But did she cry off? No! She hung in there, game to the end! Trying to make *me* cry off, you see, so Amy wouldn't be blamed! What a pair they are!"

Mr. Perry shook his head. "You are a complete hand, Barras," he said with grudging admiration. "Whatever scheme you have in mind, I shall put myself in your hands, if only it will bring me Amy! But, I must ask you, if you knew all along that Eve was masquerading as Amy, why didn't you say something earlier and save us all a great deal of trouble?"

Barras threw back his head and roared with laughter. "What? And spoil all the fun?" he then asked innocently.

Chapter
Fifteen

WHATEVER LADY SEALE SAID to her nieces, it must have been effective. But then, the dowager had the advantage of having been able to manage the Dartwood sisters into whatever plans she had arranged since their infancy. "I know what is best," had always been her refrain.

Doubtless Amy and Eve were as defenceless before her personality as Barras and Mr. Perry had been. Nor were those two gentlemen much in evidence while this interview was being conducted.

With a ruthless hand, their objections to announcing their engagements were swept aside and a picture of spinsterhood was painted that was so horrifying that even Eve had to gasp at the thought.

At one point, her maid was summoned with the

dowager's vinaigrette, and there was a most affecting scene involving vapours, recriminations and one of Lady Seale's famous heart spasms that seemed to last precisely as long as her will was being thwarted.

In the end, the twins emerged from the room, Eve pale and shaken, Amy suspiciously red-eyed, and were sent back to Dartwood House with the admonition not to be such a pair of silly, silly girls, as this was their last chance and did they want to end up a pair of ape leaders? Aunt Seale fervently hoped not!

Neither of the Dartwood twins looked at all well when they returned from their interview with Aunt Seale, but word had preceded them from the Abbey that an engagement was about to be announced. When Tallant opened the door for their return, he smiled broadly and said, in the spirit of one who has known the misses of the house since infancy, "Allow me to congratulate you both upon your happy expectations!"

Amy's reaction was to burst into tears and run up the stairs to her room, while Eve, pale but composed, managed a thin smile.

"Thank you, Tallant," she murmured, her voice stressed, "you have no idea how fortunate you are that you have never married!"

And with those words, she turned and followed her sister up the stairs, her door slamming on the heels of Amy's.

"Oh dear, whatever now?" Miss Fisher asked, appearing from the morning room.

For the first time in his long career, Tallant looked utterly human and totally astounded. "I don't know; certainly one would think that they would have been thrilled to find that all has been settled for their marriages."

"Oh, no!" Miss Fisher exclaimed involuntarily, her

final defences totally overthrown. "No! This cannot be! I must write to Sir August at once! He can, he must come home!"

She bustled off to the study in search of pen and paper, under the belief that Sir August was still in Naples, and might well have addressed him there—not that she believed it would do the least bit of good, but it would make her feel better having about discharged her duty. She had known that no good could have come from this entire escapade, and only too clearly saw that Lady Seale, in her misguided attempt to provide for her nieces' futures, had once again forced everyone's hand.

"Poor, poor, Amy," she said aloud. "And poor Eve also, for it is as clear as day that she and Mr. Perry are no more in love with each other than the man in the moon and I—"

She paused with her pen above the paper, not quite certain what to chronicle of all of this.

It was at that moment that Tallant entered the room, looking very grave indeed. "Excuse me, Miss Fisher, but Lord Barras is here, and wishes to have a word with you in particular and in private."

Miss Fisher looked up with hope in her eyes.

Chapter
Sixteen

ABOUT SEVEN THAT EVENING, Tallant left a tray outside Eve's door, assuring her through the panels that she could eat whenever she felt peckish. He added, a little fatuously, that Mrs. Beckley had sent up her favourite dessert, peach trifle. Receiving no answer, he went away shaking his head.

Save for that incident, Eve's meditations were uninterrupted, and grew darker and darker with the passing of the day into night.

A hundred times she thought up some wild scheme or another and a hundred times her fierce pride or her innate commonsense, of which she had displayed so very little in the past fortnight, asserted itself, and the scheme was cast aside.

She did not weep, but she did feel a deep despair at

the idea of being married to Mr. Perry, and a deeper despair at the idea of Amy being married to Lord Barras. It was all totally wrong and odious, and not for the first time did she mentally wish her Aunt Seale and her managing ways blown to perdition.

Like a small child sent to her room to meditate upon her transgressions, Eve had plenty of time to think, and some of the thoughts she had were not pleasant. Indeed, those who knew her would have been surprised at how many of them were entirely based upon self-reproach.

For the first time in her life, Eve Dartwood confronted her own character and what it had brought her, and she regretted it all heartily.

Although she had thrown herself across her counterpane to brood, sleep did not come at all that night. Instead, she began to have a series of increasingly disturbing revelations concerning herself, her sister, Mr. Perry, and Lord Barras.

The bell tower at Seale Abbey was just pealing out prime when Eve, still fully dressed, if slightly rumpled, rose from her bed, looking out the window at early dawn, no more than a thin pink line over the hills and hedgerows.

"Why didn't I see it all before?" she asked the dawn aloud. "Eve and Barras and Amy and Thomas! Oh, now it all makes sense, and what a capital sort of fool I have been! It has been under my nose all this time and I have been too *stupid* to see it!"

She was, of course, entirely certain that she could make the other three players in her game see the truth, too, and in her excitement, decided to immediately awaken Amy with her revelations. Not, she decided ruefully, that it would be such a grand surprise to Amy. Poor thing, she had been in love all this time, and doubtless, afraid to say a word to her twin, certain she would be stealing her sister's beau!

"Foolishness, foolishness!" Eve chuckled to herself, adding, "And *that* to Mrs. Fotherby! She'll find me a great rival indeed!"

Almost trembling with glee, Eve opened her door carefully, nearly oversetting the tray that had been left there some hours before.

The silver and china clattered loudly in the silence and Eve peered up and down the hallway, guarding herself against any unexpected appearances by housemaids, notoriously early risers.

Seeing that the coast was clear, she snuck down the hall and knocked gently on Amy's door. "Wake up, it's me," she called softly. "Come on, Amy, be a good girl and let me in."

After a moment's unfruitful search for admission, she turned the doorknob, and, somewhat to her surprise, found it unlocked.

"Amy, wake up, do," she whispered as she went into the room, "I've figured it all out, and I'm not one bit angry with you, in fact I think it's just wonderful and you should be very happy with—"

As her eyes adjusted to the dim light, her words died on her lips.

Slowly, she crossed the room and approached Amy's bed with something bordering on dread. "Amy?" she said in a wavering voice, "Amy?"

But her hand confirmed what her eyes had seen, that her sister's counterpane was smooth and unwrinkled; not so much as a valley in the featherbed betrayed any clue that Amy had been there.

Eve spun about the room, half expecting to see her

sister sprawled on the chaise or lurking in the wardrobe. "Amy?" she repeated.

She was answered only with silence. A dim feeling of panic rose up in her and was quickly suppressed. Then she saw that the window was unlatched, and indeed stood wide open to the injurious night air.

A dreadful thought seized her, and Eve rushed to the window, peering down the ivy trellis. "Amy!" she called, but the garden was silent, save for the chirping of a few early rising birds.

Anxious, Eve turned from the window again and surveyed the room, and it was only then that she saw the note pinned to the empty pillow.

Seizing upon it, Eve held it to the thin light with trembling hands, squinting as she deciphered Amy's round, diffident hand:

Dearest Eve,
  Forgive me, as I cannot go on any longer living out a Lie. I have almost stolen Thomas from you, and this is such a very Bad thing that I cannot live with you or with my own conscience any longer.
  Ld. Barras has been so kind as to offer to escape with me, and as you read this, we are on the North Rd. heading to Gretna. I know you can never, ever forgive me for the Gt. Wrong I have done you, but believe me, I am now and have always been yr. true Sister.
  Thomas is a Good man, and I know he will make you Happy. I believe that Ld. Barras will endeavour to do all in his power to make me a good Husband, and I intend to make him as good a wife as I can when my Heart belongs to Another.

                                        Adieu,
                                        Amy

Suddenly, Eve had the feeling that she knew exactly what it was to be struck by a thunderbolt. Unbelieving, she read the note again, and then a third time.

"Good Lord!" she finally exclaimed. "Oh, this is insane! She cannot! She would not!"

But, it appeared, she had.

Frantically, Eve tore back to her own room and pulled a pelisse on over her dress, tying a bonnet over her rumpled curls. From a drawer in her jewel case, she withdrew a wad of currency and stuffed it heedlessly into her reticule. She knew that it was mostly pound notes and some *lira* that would be utterly useless in this country, but in her haste, she did not care.

Stealthily, she stole down the backstairs toward the stables.

She could hear the grooms eating their breakfast in the servants' hall across the stable yard as she stole into the tack room and removed her saddle and bridle from the wall, scurrying across the stables to the stall where her favourite horse was peacefully eating her oats and gruel.

She had never saddled a horse before in her life; grooms had always abounded to do such things for her, but she did what she considered a fair enough job of the thing, crawling ungracefully into the wretched and uncomfortable sidesaddle.

She was out of the yard and halfway up the hill to Seale Abbey before anyone noticed she was gone.

Gaining entry to Seale Abbey unseen was not a problem; since childhood, she and Amy had known which window in the library never quite latched right, and how to push the frame back and forth until the catch loosened so that one could crawl into the room.

The hard part was avoiding the army of servants Lady Seale kept at her disposal. Here there was not simply one or two yawning and drowsy housemaids to watch out for, but footmen and under-butlers and stewards as well, and Eve had to duck into a shadowy alcove more than once on her way to the guest bedrooms to avoid detection.

As she wandered from room to room on the guest floor, she was aware of a certain stillness in her stealth and caution, but such considerations were far outweighed by her need for urgent stealth and secrecy. No hint, not even so much as a breath of scandal must attach to her beloved sister.

After trying several doors and finding only empty rooms, shrouded in Holland covers, Eve was so relieved to find Mr. Perry, still asleep in his gown and nightcap in the Red Room.

Rather than admiring his beauty as he slept, she ruthlessly seized his shoulder and shook him as hard as she could.

"Oh, wake up, Thomas do!" she cried in a hoarse whisper.

Mr. Perry opened one eye. He closed it again, and then, with an exclamation, sat bolt upright in bed.

"Eve!" he said in an awful voice, "What are you doing here?"

Obviously, every sense of propriety was outraged; he pulled the sheet up to his neck and glared at her in such a way as to make her drop her eyes to her toes.

"Oh, for heaven's sake," she exclaimed, coming to her senses, "there's no time for this sort of thing at all! Look at this!" From her reticule, she withdrew Amy's note and thrust it into his hand. "Read this!" she commanded.

Mr. Perry did as he was told, starting with a yawn and ending up at the bottom by saying, "Does she, by God? Well, we'll see about this! Barras goes too far!"

"Then you do love Amy?" Eve asked.

"Of course I love Amy!" Mr. Perry exclaimed, his clear blue eyes flashing. He heard himself and stopped. "Well, that is—Eve, I should have said something to you earlier about this, but—"

"No, no, no need to explain! Oh, I am relieved! I think that you two shall deal together very well indeed, and I wish you both well! I think you and I are far more suited to be brother and sister than husband and wife, and now I must prevent Amy from doing something so obviously stupid! Whatever can Barras have been thinking about, to elope with her like that? The scandal will be dreadful unless we can stop them and bring them back home at once! Dearest Amy, she meant well, but I fear that I am not worthy of such a sacrifice!"

"Nor shall I allow her to do so! When Barras said he had a plan, I did not think he meant this!"

"You mean that he knew what he was doing?"

"He knew about you all along! That you were not Amy, but Eve!"

"Odious, odious man! And this, I see, is how he intends to pay me back! Was there ever a man more odious? Well, if he thinks he can kidnap my sister away from here—there are laws, are there not, about abducting heiresses?"

"Yes, but I don't think they apply to Lord Barras! He is as rich as a nabob and Amy only has five hundred a year," Mr. Perry pointed out commonsensically.

It was that remark that reminded Eve precisely what annoyed her the most about Mr. Perry; his willingness to quibble almost any point. She would have told him so, but realised, wisely at last, if late, that further bickering would only delay Amy's rescue.

"And besides, if he means to escape me, he has another thought coming! He should know that he loves me, not Amy!" Eve exclaimed aloud.

"For God's sake, Eve, keep your voice down or you'll have the entire household in here, and then we will have a scandal!"

"We'll have one anyway, if we do not stop Barras on the Great North Road!" Eve exclaimed with spirit. "What do you intend to do? Lie in bed all day while the woman you love elopes with the man I love?"

"I knew it was April and May between you and Barras!" Mr. Perry expostulated. "I knew it all along!"

"Yes, it was and it is, and what crackbrained scheme has he dreamed up now, winnowing Amy away to Gretna Green? That serves no purpose at all!"

"Well, if you would leave the room, I might be able to get dressed, although I really should ring for my valet—"

"This is a rescue mission, not a stroll down Bond Street! Thomas, I often wonder where your priorities are!"

Nonetheless, she waited in the hall until he emerged, fully dressed and ready to give chase.

"I thought my brown fustian coat would do," he said dubiously, drawing on his gloves. "I assume you have arranged for a vehicle? Pursuing a high-perch phaeton and a spirited team of four high steppers is going to be some job of work, you know."

"Especially with the lead they must have on us! Happily, his left leader is a mite touched in the wind, and the team will have to be changed by the time they reach Great Cross, so we may expect there to be delays!"

"It sounds wonderful," Mr. Perry said, sighing, "but what about our team?"

"Well, I thought you could take something from Aunt Seale's stable. Unfortunately, cousin Timothy's got his phaeton down in London, but there is a curricle—"

"And what am I supposed to say to the grooms? Hello, I'm off to chase Lord Barras, who's eloping with my intended wife, and I need to borrow Lady Seale's curricle for the purpose?"

"Don't say anything to them! Just give them the order!" Eve commanded, growing increasingly more exasperated with each passing moment.

"Yes, of course!"

"And then we'll have your aunt all over us, and I don't know about you, but Lady Seale is not a female I would wish to cross! A rare to-do there will be when she gets wind of all this!"

"That is precisely the point! She must not get wind of all of this!" Eve said, exasperation turning into a rank impatience. "Oh, why did I ever even think of marrying you? You are so—so poetical!"

"And you are a hoyden! I might remind you that if it had not been for you, none of this would have happened, you know!"

Speechless with irritation, Eve gripped his arm and dragged Perry back into the alcove, as a housemaid bearing an armload of sheets entered the corridor and walked past them down the passage.

"There is no use wasting any time with you!" Eve said once the maid was out of sight. "I'll see to it myself."

"You do that!" Mr Perry muttered. "Of all the corkbrained schemes—it was you who led us all into this pother, you know!"

"I know," Eve said with a sigh. "I know, and now I have my chance to repent! But if they think they will escape us, they are a great deal mistaken!"

Mr. Perry believed her.

The sun was rising over the fields as the curricle, drawn by a team of four respectable, if not precisely sporty horses set out to bounce up the Great North Road in search of the missing couple.

Stops at the various hamlets along the way elicited little or no information on a couple in a high-perch phaeton with yellow wheels, and a female who looked like Eve.

"They must have come through in the middle of the night when everyone was asleep!" Eve said. "How annoying of them! They cannot have gotten past Banbury, though, without a change of horses!"

"Nor, I fear, shall we!" Mr. Perry exclaimed. "The pin seems to be loose in the right rear axle."

"That is because you are the most ham-handed driver I have ever seen in my life!" Eve cried indignantly. She peered behind the vehicle and looked at the wheel. It did, indeed, seem to be wobbling, but not a great deal.

"Ham-handed! I suppose you could do better! You very nearly killed us that time in Italy with your driving!" Mr. Perry snapped.

"I did not! That was a simple miscalculation!"

Nerves, it was very clear, were fraying dreadfully as they made their way up the road.

Now that the morning was advancing, the highway was growing more crowded with traffic, and it was all that Mr. Perry could do to avoid a collision with a green-grocer's cart that had suddenly pulled out into the lane from behind a hedge directly in their path.

"That was close! Why don't you pay attention to where you're going? Thomas, if we don't catch him, all will be lost!"

"It's a long way to Gretna Green," Mr. Perry retorted. "A very long way indeed, and if you don't settle down, I shall be forced to go against all my principles and throttle you *long* before we reach Northampton! Poor Amy! It is only the thought of her that sustains me!"

Eve pulled her hat down very low on her head and crossed her arms over her chest, wondering what she had ever seen in this man.

Mr. Perry was wondering what he had ever seen in Eve at the same time, so that they were able to ride along for quite a number of miles without exchanging words. The landscape seemed to sail past them in a blur of green, through the necklace of small towns on the road between the south and the north. At each likely looking inn, they paused only long enough to inquire after Lord Barras and Miss Amy Dartwood, but no one seemed to have seen them pass.

They had changed horses once without stopping for a rest themselves at Banbury, and after some inquiry, it was discovered that an 'ostler at the Blue Swan recalled Lord Barras's phaeton and team, if not his passenger and person.

"Bang up to the knocker thet was!" he exclaimed, after Mr. Perry had greased his fist with a cartwheel. "All bays and all matched, right down to the blaze in the forehead! But I dunno about none o' the people, see, it were early in the morning, and I was awake half the night with a spavined hoss!"

"Well, at least we know we are not more than an hour or so behind them," Perry said as they took to the road again.

"Even that may be too late! But at least we know he has to change teams soon." Eve replied. "That will slow him down, and Amy gets travel sick, so he'll have to stop for *that* once or twice along the way."

Miss Dartwood's tart observation that Mr. Perry was not a good driver was only partially true. Knowing his own limitations, he wisely used care and caution in his handling of the team, but Eve, who was a neck-or-nothing type, stewed and fretted almost constantly, anxious to catch up with Lord Barras, whom she knew to be complete to a shade of utter recklessness, when pressed to the point. Mr. Perry, on the other hand, having no great interest in the sport and being concerned only with getting himself from one place to the other, was a mere whipster.

When Thomas drew in behind the slow and lumbering Northern Flyer Mail Coach, although he had what Eve described tersely as *yards and yards* to spare between himself and an oncoming oxcart, she almost saw red.

"You'd better let *me* drive," she said impetuously, and started to wrest the reins from his hands.

Unfortunately, Mr. Perry had other ideas, and resisted her strongly. "I say, Eve! Don't do that!" he shouted, but it was too late.

Sensing that for a moment no one was in control, the horses spread in the shafts and shied away from the dust left behind by the Flyer.

"We're going into the ditch!" Eve screamed, just as the loose pin in the axle, finally strained to its breaking point, separated from the axle. The curricle spun dizzily out of control and into a ditch, where it piled up on one side, its free wheels spinning crazily.

Eve found herself pulled out into the grassy bank of the ditch, the breath knocked out of her, but otherwise unhurt—save for her pride, which was severely damaged.

She had taken worse spills in her life and was on her feet in an instant, seeing to the horses.

"I like your fine priorities," Mr. Perry said as he crawled out from beneath the seat, unhurt but rubbing his backside somewhat ruefully. "We could have been killed!"

"Horses are always a priority over people," Eve retorted, "and you ought to be glad that they are not hurt, you know."

Mr. Perry straightened up and glared at her fiercely. "By God," he said, his poetic soul moved to deep tones of loathing, "I shall forever be glad that I did not marry you! Hoydenish, harebrained, sporting creature!"

"And I share your sentiments exactly! You are the worst ham-fisted whipster I have ever seen in my life!"

"Well, it was you who grabbed the reins from my hands—you might have killed us both!"

"Oh, be quiet, do," Eve hissed. "People are coming and they are bound to talk."

Half an hour later (a precious half hour, Eve kept thinking, in which Barras had yet more time to reach the North) they were at the White Stag in Five Points Cross. While Perry went in search of a blacksmith to repair the wheel of the curricle, Eve, sadly disheveled and dirty, made arrangements with the landlord for the stabling and resting of Lady Seale's horses.

"By the way," she added, almost as an afterthought, "have you seen a gentleman in a curricle together with a lady who looked a great deal like me pass this way?"

When Mr. Perry reappeared upon the scene a quarter hour later, still rubbing at the dust that had been ground into his pearl-grey jacket, it was to find Eve, hair tangled, pelisse filthy and fire in her eye, pacing up and down in front of the inn.

"The smith says he can have it fixed by this afternoon, but I had to bribe him with a coachwheel to take me over Farmer Glossop's cart."

Eve looked up at him woefully. "They are in Stratford-on-Avon," she said.

Mr. Perry stared at her for a moment, as if she had run quite mad.

"Barras and my sister are in Stratford-on-Avon. At the Mermaid Inn, if you can believe such a thing," she repeated, listlessly picking lint off her skirt.

"Stratford-on-Avon?" Mr. Perry repeated, a little confused. "But that isn't even on the Great North Road. What in the world are they doing in Stratford?"

Eve shook her head. "I really don't know, but I think, I really do think that when I catch up with Gervase Barras, I am going to render his life so entirely unpleasant that he will regret this day for the rest of his life. I almost died when the landlord here told me that they had passed this way this morning and booked a private parlour for breakfast. Whatever is he up to? Can't he even manage a simple elopement?" Eve was whining and she knew it, but she also knew she could not stop, so she said nothing more for several moments. For his part, Mr. Perry pondered this statement with his usual thoroughness.

"Well, then, I suppose that it falls to us to procure some sort of transportation and proceed on to Stratford," he concluded.

Eve nodded. "There is the landlord's gig, which he has agreed to rent us for the afternoon. Can you imagine what a sight we shall be, arriving in a gig?"

"It hardly bears thinking of," Mr. Perry said with the utmost sincerity.

"Nonetheless, we must get there before he ruins Amy's reputation—*or* worse entirely!" Eve said with a great deal of conviction. "There may not a moment to lose!"

The Mermaid was a pleasant hostelry of waddle and ersatz thatch, such as might have existed in Stratford in

Shakespeare's day, had it not been built by a canny builder some ten years earlier to satisfy the tourist's demand for all things Tudor.

It was not the most prestigious inn in Stratford, but it was clean and respectable, and when a gig bearing a very dusty couple, he with mud-splattered driving cape and she with a decidedly crumpled appearance, drove into the yard, the landlady was tempted to tell them to seek accommodations elsewhere, as she had none to give.

But she was engaged in chasing a fat capon around the yard, and was hardly prepared for the urgency with which Eve accosted her, looking somewhat like a madwoman in her crumpled hat.

"Quick—have you seen a very tall blond man and a ginger-haired female who looks very much like me today! I must know!" Eve exclaimed, barely waiting for Mr. Perry to bring the gig to a halt before she jumped out and confronted the landlady.

As bedraggled as she might have been, her accents were still Quality, as the landlady would say later, but what was truly shocking was her remarkable resemblance to the other young lady in the private parlour. At first she thought it was the same person, but as she had just seen the other lady go into the inn, she knew this could not be so.

"Twins!" she exclaimed in tones of satisfaction. "You're her twin, aren't you?"

Eve nodded. "Is she here?" she asked urgently.

The landlady nodded. "Why, they've bespoke the best parlour in the house and a supper besides—" she started to say, but Eve had dashed away and into the common room before she could finish her sentence, leaving Mr. Perry behind with his full purse and ready explanation.

The inn was abustle; it was high tourist season in the birthplace of the Bard, and the added excitement of Quality folk such as the inn had never seen before was almost more than could be stood; fresh chickens for dinner and the landlady's very best apple tarts, and the hired boy sent over to Bricoe Farm to see if sausages could be obtained for the gentleman's dinner, and the good wine dragged up from the cellar where it had lain these many years, and now this odd, dusty and bedraggled couple coming after the first set, who had seemed like such nice people.

"If that's Quality, you may give me plain business people," the landlady confided to her barmaid. "Far too eccentric for the likes of us!"

Eve threw open the door of the parlour and stood in the threshold, an avenging wraith. "If you thought I wouldn't track the pair of you down, you are very much wrong!" she exclaimed.

Lord Barras lounged comfortably in a chair, one long leg thrown over the other, a glass of stout at his elbow, while Amy, looking very fetching in a sprig muslin gown, sat daintily in the other chair, looking up at her sister with just a hint of mischief in her eyes.

Between them a chessboard was laid out on the table, and Barras was in the act of checking Amy's pawn.

They both looked up at her as if she had been expected, and she was suddenly, and for an instant only, acutely aware of her smudged and rumpled appearance, knowing that she must look a sight and a fright.

"Evelina Dartwood! Have you been jauntering about the country dressed in such a fashion?" said a familiar voice, and Eve turned to behold Miss Fisher seated by the cold fireplace, a piece of needlework in her hand. She suddenly felt dizzy. "Tabby? I do not understand!"

"Miss Fisher was good enough to lend us her company on this journey to Stratford," Lord Barras drawled. "I had a fancy, you see, to visit the birthplace of the Bard, and your sister was good enough to offer to accompany me. We have seen Anne Hathaway's cottage and Will's burial place and a great deal more besides, and now we are waiting to have a little luncheon before we venture forth again."

"But you said—Amy, you said you were eloping with Gervase! But Tabby is here!"

Amy did not hear her sister, for at that moment Mr. Perry appeared behind Eve. Without a word, Amy rose from her seat and drifted toward him, her eyes alive, her hands outstretched. In his presence, she was utterly and beautifully radiant, and Eve watched, nonplussed as she joined hands with Mr. Perry and they drifted, oblivious to the rest of the world, out into the sunshine.

She stared after them for quite some moments, her breath rising and falling in her bosom, before she was aware that Lord Barras was chuckling.

"So, you fell into my trap! But it looks as if you have fallen into someone's trap earlier today! Did you overturn the gig?"

Eve could only nod. "I am deplorably ham-handed. It was a *stupid* accident and I am to—" she broke off, her expression becoming dark and stormy as she stared at Barras's crooked smile, mocking her as he lounged in his chair. "Horrible man," she said softly, and then she began to laugh.

All the tension she had been experiencing for the past weeks dissolved, and, weak in the knees, she sank into the chair Amy had vacated and shook her head, tears rolling down her cheeks.

"You knew! You know I am *Eve,* not Amy!" she exclaimed. "Oh, Gervase, you are horrible!"

"Almost as horrible as you! But I am very glad you are not hurt—really, Eve, you are a dashed ham-handed girl!"

"We lost an axle pin and spilled into a ditch. But the horses are all right," she said, laughing.

"And, knowing you, you saw to them immediately."

"Of course. Thomas was *furious!* Gervase, I think it is obvious that he and I are as ill-suited as day and night!"

"I was wondering if you had reached that conclusion yet," Barras said, rising from his chair and going to stand over her, his hands thrust into his pockets.

"I think," Miss Fisher said tactfully, "that I shall go and tell the landlady that we shall be two more for lunch."

But neither Barras nor Eve heard her as she slipped quietly from the room, a serene smile on her face for the first time in weeks.

Eve stopped laughing. She looked up at Barras. Barras looked down at her. "There is a great deal I could and should say to you," he started, reaching down and seizing her by the wrists, dragging her to her feet, and peering down at her from beneath his heavy quizzical brows, his dark eyes flashing. "But I think if I said it now, you and I should never be properly married as we should be, and that is something I cannot bear."

"But—" Eve said.

She was cut off by a sudden and ruthless kiss that made her decide it was best to keep silent for the time being, but after a while, she could not suppress a gurgle of laughter.

"Deplorable levity! It is one of your sins!" he

growled, still holding her very tightly against him. "And one that I shall always cherish."

"You did me, just as I did you! I guess we are even now!" Eve managed to say.

"And I mean it to stay that way! From now on, we run neck and neck, not fore and aft, do you hear?"

Eve nodded. "Neck and neck, whatever the field!" she promised.

Barras looked down at her fiercely. Seemingly satisfied, he nodded. "I have lured your papa back to Oxford by promising him the Etruscan goddess as a part of my settlement," he said. "And yes, I knew that was you at Westerby's that day! In fact I've thought it was you since the first time you opened your mouth! You and your sister may fool others, but you are as different to me as chalk and cheese. Now when Sir August arrives, I shall ask him for his blessing, and we shall be married as soon as I can procure a special licence! I have no intention of allowing you to run loose any longer than I have to, else who knows what trouble you might land us in?"

"Yes," Eve said breathlessly. She wanted to be kissed again, and Barras obliged her roundly.

When at last he let go, she laid her head against his chest and sighed. "I wonder what Aunt Seale will say?" she asked.

"No doubt she will be heartily relieved that you are someone else's responsibility!" Lord Barras pronounced.